UNDERCOVER TRUCKER (An American Mystery)

By Lance Majestik

UNDERCOVER TRUCKER (An American Mystery)

TABLE OF CONTENTS

CHAPTER 1 (Commitment Phobia)

I've been cursed with some sort of commitment repellant ever since I was in high school.

That impediment was inextricably intertwined in just about every aspect of my life.

As a result, at age thirty-three, I've never been married, shacked up with a chick or even dated a girl for longer than a few months.

I've changed careers mid-stream more times than I can even count, much to the chagrin of my parents.

My two older sisters and one much older brother are all high achievers solidly immersed in lucrative careers. I'm the exception.

My folks are exceedingly well-to-do. They're fully retired and spent much of their time travelling the world until the Covid-19 pandemic hit.

Now they split their time between their summer home in the

Thousand Islands and their winter residence in Arizona.

I guess I'm the recipient of what is trendily being called white privilege although in reality it should be termed the privilege of wealth because my situation has nothing to do with skin color.

By the way, my name is Benton Marcotte.

Today is Friday, the 23rd of October, 2020 and I just watched my folks board their flight in Syracuse which will take them to Phoenix, Arizona for their winter sojourn.

For the time being I'll reside in their Alexandria Bay, New York residence.

As has happened so often over the past fifteen years, I'm in between jobs and have no further university courses scheduled.

On the face of it, my résumé is quite impressive.

From September of 2005 until early April of 2009 I attended State University of New York at the Syracuse campus on a full karate scholarship. I had won several tournaments during my high school years. At first I intended to open a martial arts dojo and majored in philosophy but lost interest in that career goal at the end of my second year so I switched majors to business and received my Honors Bachelor of Commerce degree two years later.

I lived at my parents' home during those four university years in order to keep my living costs down.

For the next year I was employed at a stock broker's office in Albany, New York but found the work uninspiring.

From September of 2010 until June of 2012 I worked for an accounting firm in Watertown, New York while taking various required courses and obtained my Certified Public Accountant designation during that period.

Unable to commit myself to the boring life of an accountant, I took a year off and drove around

North America in my trusty old automobile, spending a week or two here and there while taking in the scenic points of interest of the various sections of the USA, Canada and even a bit of Mexico.

That extended holiday enabled me to contemplate my future and I decided to become a lawyer.

I managed a partial scholarship for law school tuition and used some of my accumulated savings to tide me over for the next three years while I earned my JD at SUNY in Rochester, New York.

Surprisingly, I never needed to borrow any money from my parents or to take out any student loans.

After passing the New York State bar exams in July of 2016, I toiled for the next two years at a large law firm in Rochester but loathed the job.

My salary and bonuses had been quite generous and I managed to save up a lot of money. The obscene work hours prevented me from having any kind of social life. The entire two years were spent in the office or sleeping. Working fourteen plus hours each day including weekends was about as close to slavery as a young guy could ever experience.

After a month of sloth, I decided that I wanted to be a doctor.

A medical school in Buffalo accepted my application and I fully expected to begin training for my new career in September of 2018 until I was hit by an epiphany that I got queasy at the mere sight of blood.

Besides, churning through dozens of boring but worried patients each day would soon become tedious.

I wisely withdrew my application and gave up on my brief dream of being a physician.

From October of 2018 until last week I drove a transport truck, having obtained my applicable driver's training and licence in less than a month.

Toiling in a blue collar job had its own advantages and drawbacks but I enjoyed the solitary time on the highways.

My parents were predictably disgusted with that temporary choice of career and my reputation as the black sheep of the family was further solidified.

Really it was none of their business. Despite my parents' significant wealth, I never borrowed a single dollar from them. I was quite proud of the fact that I was totally independent.

As a matter of fact my unusual status amused me while I was hauling freight around the country.

Benton Marcotte for that brief period of time was unique, the only guy in the trucking industry with a Bachelor of Commerce, CPA and JD all rolled into one confused and overeducated specimen.

The small trucking company I worked for was bought out and the new bosses were not generous employers. I turned down their insulting offer to continue working for them.

I'm certainly not unique now. I'm just one of perhaps twelve million guys out of work during the Covid-19 rape of the American economy.

I guess I could now accurately be described as an unpaid house-sitter for my parents' summer home.

I don't have a clue what to do with my life right now but my choices are many. I've kept up my membership dues and mandatory continuing education courses with both my accounting and legal professions.

CHAPTER 2 (Uncle Don)

I made it back to Alexandria Bay shortly after noon. I still drive a 2003 Chevrolet Malibu which I had purchased in 2008 from an elderly lady whose eyesight had failed her to the extent that she was no longer able to drive.

She sold me the vehicle at a great price with the condition that for one full year I would drive her to the grocery store each week and also take her to the occasional medical appointment.

My parents had criticized my vehicle ever since I bought it. They believed that one's automobile should reflect your status and pedigree in life. Since I resided in their home at the time, they complained often about the embarrassment of having such an ordinary automobile parked in plain sight on their property.

Despite their abhorrence of my car, they nevertheless allowed me to drive them to the Syracuse airport today because they were worried that a limousine service might have been too unreliable and they didn't want to miss their flight. Escaping the cold New York winters was a high priority for them.

There's one more aspect of my personality that I should disclose.

Because of my stubborn independent streak, I had a tendency to be sarcastic or downright caustic with other folks.

Benton Marcotte was a classic smart-ass.

That probably explained at least partially why I couldn't maintain a relationship with a woman or even develop close friendships with other guys.

My martial arts skills prevented me from getting my ass kicked when I mouthed off.

My size was also a deterrent for alpha males. I was six feet three inches tall and a rather muscular 245 pounds.

One of my more recent resolutions was to tone down my snarky comments and not feel compelled to throw in my two cents worth at every opportunity.

As I had learned repeatedly over the past several years, no one likes a know-it-all.

I fully realized that I was a bit too solitary for my own good. That's likely the reason I enjoyed the life of a long-distance trucker despite the lack of folks with which to converse about various topics. I was being paid to live the life of a loner and had plenty of time to contemplate the weighty issues of a complex world as well as to introspect about my own personality.

On Saturday morning I was working out in my parents' exercise room when their phone rang.

It was Uncle Don, my mother's younger brother.

"I'm surprised to reach you, Benny. I thought you were still driving the big rigs much to the disgust of my snobbish older sister."

My uncle was the only one in the family to shorten my given name. Everyone else called me Benton because my parents insisted on it. In actual fact I loathed the name Benton. Uncle Don was a rebel, a bit like me I guess.

"My employer was bought out about a week ago and the new owner wanted to maximize profit at the expense of its drivers. I rejected their offer and decided to seek my fame and fortune elsewhere. I'm staying here temporarily while I figure out my next adventure."

"What are your options?"

"I've kept my accounting and lawyer's licences up-to-date so I may opt to open up my own CPA business or legal office."

"Do you have the capital to do that?"

"I've been very thrifty of late and have managed to accumulate a decent nest-egg but I'm not sure if I'd really enjoy running my own business in either of those professions. I'm even toying with the idea of trying something completely different."

"Well, I wish you all the best, Benny. Is Gabriela available to speak with me?"

"No she's not. I drove her and Dad to the Syracuse airport yesterday. They should be ensconced in their Maricopa winter home by now. Do you have their Arizona phone number?"

"Yes I do. I may call her later. It's too early in Arizona right now. All I was going to do was moan to her about one of my factories."

"What's the problem? Are the Covid-19 restrictions hurting your business?"

"They're not helping, that's for sure, but I've got a smallish operation in the tiny town of Wellsville in the southwestern section of Upper New York State. The facility is losing money and I wanted to discuss with your mother what obstacles she faced when she closed down that chocolate factory in Utica just before she and your Dad retired."

"Aren't you paying high-priced lawyers and accountants for that sort of advice?"

"Of course I do but those outfits are all cut-throat bottom-line fanatics. My sister has a conscience and might be able to give me more compassionate advice. Shutting down my operation will throw about thirty-five folks out of work in a town without many replacement jobs and during this pandemic."

"Have your accountants analyzed why the plant is losing money?"

"They've looked at the numbers but were unable to pinpoint any specific reasons for the drop in profits other than the fact that both product lines have been stagnant or declining."

"Did they send an efficiency expert to Wellsville to oversee the actual factory?"

"No. They just recommended that I close it up."

"I'm not otherwise occupied right now. Would you like me to head down to Wellsville and snoop around for you?"

"That's a tempting offer. Perhaps you can put some of that expensive education to good use."

Uncle Don and I discussed the specifics of how I would worm my way into the factory.

He felt that placing me in the accounting department wouldn't allow me to get a real feel for the entire operation and he already knew pretty much all he needed to know about the actual sales and overhead numbers.

He said that he'd call me back shortly after he'd spoken with the plant manager.

My uncle called back fifteen minutes later.

"There's only one opening at the plant right now, Benny, but it might be right up your alley. Their truck driver just quit without any notice. Are you willing to fill that spot in the shipping department at the factory in order to fly under the radar? It only pays $18 an hour."

"That will do nicely to keep me temporarily occupied."

Uncle Don believed that as an ordinary Joe working on the factory floor, I could get a much more accurate feel about the operation.

I agreed to drive today to Uncle Don's home in Rochester which was about one hundred and seventy-five miles southwest of Alexandria Bay. He would provide me with all the accounting information he had amassed about the Wellsville factory and we could go over the numbers tonight.

Tomorrow I would drive the final seventy-five miles to Wellsville.

I arrived at Uncle Don's home at three o'clock. He was a widower with no kids and had never even dated anyone after his wife died several years ago.

He gave me a laptop computer on which he had downloaded the

factory's financial summaries and assorted other information about the business.

The plant manufactured kitty litter and clay bricks. As such it had been deemed to be an essential service and had been able to operate throughout the Covid-19 lockdowns, albeit with various restrictions such as masks and social distancing.

Uncle Don admitted that his hope was that the factory could be saved. He hated the thought of firing so many employees a month or two before Christmas.

I promised him that I'd do my best to evaluate the operation accurately and let him know if the plant could be salvaged.

This temporary gig lifted my spirits considerably. Evaluating the workings of a small manufacturing facility would be another notch on my already long belt of jobs.

CHAPTER 3 (Hello Wellsville)

Uncle Don and I went out to a diner for a leisurely breakfast after which I left for Wellsville which was actually both a village and a town. The town portion encircled the original village and the combined population was about 7,200.

I had never lived in such a small place.

My parents resided in Syracuse when I was growing up and subsequently I had lived there and in Rochester, Watertown and Albany. Of those cities, Watertown was the smallest with a population of about 30,000. I had never lived at my parents' Alexandria Bay home although I very occasionally stayed there with them for very short visits.

For this undercover assignment, my uncle and I had decided that I would use my first name, Robert in order to avoid anyone figuring out from the internet or elsewhere that Benton Marcotte possessed advanced university degrees. My Dad's name was Robert and Mom had decided to call me by my middle name in order to avoid confusion in our household.

We also decided not to tell anyone in the factory, in Uncle Don's accounting or legal departments, or even my parents what he and I were up to.

My uncle simply wanted my report on the impact on Wellsville of the factory closure if that's what he decided to do.

He purposely hadn't provided any information to the plant manager. He had simply made some general inquiries about the factory and ascertained by chance that the factory's truck driver had unexpectedly quit on Friday. Uncle Don had used that tidbit of information as his opening to insert me into the factory and informed the manager that he would fill the position with the son of a friend who was a certified driver and happened to be between jobs at the moment. Uncle Don had called the manager back a bit later and provided him with my pertinent details so that I could begin employment on Monday morning.

I called the caretaker of my parents' summer home and let him know that I was leaving Alexandria Bay already.

Then I called Mom but only informed her that I had accepted another trucking job in the western section of New York. She was suitably appalled and harangued me for a solid twenty minutes about my lack of responsibility and maturity.

I was glad when we ended the call.

It took me just under two hours to reach Wellsville.

I drove around the town first to get a feel for the place and then I located the factory which was about a mile north of town on a rural concession road.

Back in Wellsville, I drove up and down many of the streets looking for apartment rental signs.

In a somewhat run-down old wooden home with an unkempt yard, I spotted a faded homemade sign announcing that there was a furnished one-bedroom apartment for rent.

Even though it was Sunday, I rang the front doorbell and opted not to wear my face mask although I was holding it in my hand just in case it was needed. An elderly lady came to the door and she wasn't wearing a mask either.

"Hello, ma'am; my name's Bobby Marcotte and I'll be starting work at the kitty litter factory tomorrow. I just arrived in Wellsville and happened to notice the FURNISHED APARTMENT FOR RENT sign in your front window. Is it still available?"

"Yes it is. I'm Gertrude Salisbury. When would you want to move in?"

"I could pay you the rent in cash today and move in immediately. That would save me from having to find a motel room."

"Do you have references?"

"I'm afraid not. For the past two years I've been employed as a long distance trucker and generally lived in my vehicle or in motels."

"Are you a smoker?"

"No I'm not and I can assure you that I've very quiet and responsible, but I do have a car so I'll need a parking spot."

"The apartment is at the rear and up a steep set of stairs. It's been vacant since August when my grandson passed away. He had lived there for several years."

"I'll need to know how much the rent is before I commit myself. I also don't want to sign a lease just in case the job doesn't work out well."

"I want to receive $160 per week but that rent includes utilities since the apartment isn't metered separately from the main house."

"That rent is satisfactory. Can I see the unit first just to make sure that it will suit my needs?"

"Of course you may. I'll get you a key. I hurt my leg in a fall last month so I'm no longer able to navigate the rear staircase."

"That's no problem, Mrs. Salisbury. I'll take a look at the apartment and come right back to let you know whether I'd like to rent it from you."

The woman retrieved an apartment key and I walked around to the rear of the building.

The stairs were quite steep and not in very good repair but the unit itself was quite appealing. The bedroom, bathroom and kitchen were small but the living-room was a nice size and the carpet was stain-free. The furniture was very basic but appeared to be in reasonably good condition.

It would serve me well for the time being since I only expected to reside in Wellsville until the end of the year.

I walked around to the front door and advised the lady that I'd be pleased to rent the apartment from her.

I inquired if the apartment had been hooked up to the internet and she replied that it still was. Mrs. Salisbury used her own computer and her service had also covered the apartment because her grandson used his own computer up there. Cable TV was also hooked up and included in my rent.

She didn't require a damage deposit or any prepaid rent but I paid her $800 to cover the rent for five weeks. She provided me with a receipt and I kept the key she had loaned me.

We agreed that either of us could terminate the tenancy on seven days' notice.

For the next hour I moved my belongings into my new digs. I had only brought two business suits and left the rest of my office wardrobe at my parents' house. In fact I hadn't even worn a suit for almost two years.

Next I drove around town again and purchased some groceries and beer.

The apartment was equipped with pots and pans, cutlery, towels, sheets and a blanket so there weren't any household items that I needed to purchase. There was even a coffee maker and a toaster in the kitchen.

I was pleased with my rapid progress. Finding suitable accommodation in less than an hour was a real bonus.

After cooking my own supper, I turned on the television and watched cable news for the evening.

The presidential election was happening in just nine days and the news was dominated by that event plus Covid-19 new case numbers.

CHAPTER 4 (Buxton Manufacturing)

On Monday morning I showered, dressed in work clothes and work boots, hopped in my car and drove to Buxton Manufacturing which was the name of Uncle Don's factory.

Uncle Don's surname was Adamson and he had left the factory name unchanged when he purchased the business from the Buxton family twelve years ago.

Many sets of eyes were following me as I walked from my car in the employees' lot to the front door of the factory where I spotted the personnel office.

Once inside, the three women all seemed to be staring at me. It was a bit off-putting. I approached the counter.

"Good morning. My name's Bobby Marcotte and I've been hired to start today in the shipping room. I thought I'd better stop at personnel first in case there's some paperwork that needs to be dealt with."

"No one's told me about any new hire. Who were you speaking with?"

"I made the arrangements on-line and just arrived in Wellsville yesterday."

The woman typed away on her computer for a moment and looked up at me.

"There's no record of you here. I guess you've been scammed but there's nothing I can do to assist you."

She turned her back on me and began working on one of her files.

It was incredibly rude.

"Why don't you try the name Robert Marcotte? Bobby's just the name I go by. In case you're only semi-literate, I'll also spell my surname for you."

I spelled out Marcotte slowly letter by letter.

The woman swung to face me and she was blushing either from embarrassment or anger. Her eyes were blazing which indicated that she was enraged at my insolence.

I chastised myself for being so aggressive but the woman's behavior had appalled me.

She yelled to a co-worker.

"Marcie, look after this guy. I'm busy."

A younger woman asked me to move over to her section of the counter closer to her computer. There were plastic barriers separating the employees from the customer area.

Within a few seconds she had located my details on her machine.

"I've got you, Bobby. We've already got your Social Insurance Number and other necessary details in our system. There's nothing else we require. You can access the shipping room by exiting at the main door and turning left. Continue around to the west side of the building."

"Thank you, miss."

I did as she had instructed and found myself at the shipping bays. I entered the side door and looked around.

"You're not allowed in here," a young guy bellowed.

Already I was learning that there were no proper customer relations at the plant. This was the second worker who'd been dismissive.

"I'm the new employee. Where's the supervisor?"

He yelled for someone named Brian who appeared almost immediately.

"I'm Brian Kirkwood. How may I help you?"

"My name's Bobby Marcotte. I'm your new truck driver and general assistant."

"Welcome aboard, Bobby. That was quick. Carl only quit on Friday morning. Do you have all the required licences?"

"I do. I've been a long-distance truck driver for the past two years."

Brian asked to see my Commercial Driver's Licence which I produced from my wallet.

"That's great. Our own truck is already loaded with kitty litter bound for Olean, Jamestown and Lackawanna. The addresses for the deliveries are on the manifest. I'm thrilled that you've shown up this morning. I thought I was going to have to make the run myself."

To assist me, Brian handed me a detailed map of the delivery locations in each drop.

I hopped in the cab and headed out on the road. The total run was about 200 miles and I was expected to be back to the plant before four-thirty when the place closed.

The deliveries were a piece of cake and I had no difficulty finding the customers or having the respective cargo off-loaded.

I made it back to Buxton Manufacturing at three o'clock.

Brian was very pleased because it gave him time to show me tomorrow's cargo run which hit Elmira, Ithaca and Rochester.

Brian explained that those were the only two kitty litter runs each week.

The clay brick end of the business was quiet at the moment and wouldn't likely pick up until spring. The bricks manufactured at the factory were used mostly in the construction of fireplaces and specialty kilns. Occasionally over the late fall and winter there might be a brick order that needed to be delivered and some of those customers were much further afield.

The closing whistle sounded and my first day on the job was over.

I hadn't learned much except that the head lady in the office was a bitch. Brian had mentioned that Gordie, the young chap in the shipping room was a bit simple which explained his lack of manners.

Brian was pleasant and had an aura of competence about him. I hoped that tomorrow or Wednesday he'd have an opportunity to give me a tour of the plant.

CHAPTER 5 (Second Day, First Fight)

I drove home and made supper.

Tomorrow would be another busy day on the road so I spent the evening studying tomorrow's delivery route and then the financial records summary that Uncle Don had provided to me.

Tuesday was a rainy and rather miserable day on the highways and the deliveries didn't progress as smoothly as yesterday. At two of the drop locations I had to wait for an offloading bay to become available and that wasted a fair bit of time.

As a result I didn't make it back to the factory until shortly after closing time although I had called Brian to let him know why I was going to be late. He instructed me to keep the truck keys and bring them in tomorrow.

As I parked the truck and began walking to my car, two men were arguing with another chap. They knocked him to the ground at which point I decided to intervene.

"What's going on here?" I bellowed.

"It's none of your business, fat boy. Get the fuck out of here before we kick the shit out of you too."

"That's not going to happen, pal. Do you even work here?"

"Damn right I do."

By then I was within ten feet of the men and they could see unless they were morons that I didn't have an ounce of fat on me. That apparently made no difference.

"Leave the gentleman alone and get off the property now. I won't ask you twice."

Both men standing were big bruisers and they immediately turned their attention on me.

It dawned on me that I was going to get into a fight on only my second day on the job.

They rushed me using the normally reasonable premise that

two against one was an absolute guarantee of success.

My left foot drove upwards and connected with the right side of my first opponent's face. Immediately upon impact I regained my balance and faced the second assailant who had wisely stopped his forward progress.

"It's your funeral, asshole. I'd prefer not to hurt you as well because you'll need to lug your friend home once he regains consciousness. I don't want to leave the two of you here on the pavement to freeze to death overnight."

He raised his hands in a gesture of surrender.

I looked down at their victim who was still on the ground.

"Are you okay?"

"I guess so. Thanks for stepping in."

I directed my gaze at the second assailant.

"Do you need a hand carrying the corpse to your vehicle?"

"That would make it a lot easier."

Together we lifted the first chap up and put one of our shoulders under each of his arms.

By the time we'd hauled him to a beat-up old car, he was regaining consciousness. We eased his body onto the back seat and laid him down as best we could.

The second fellow got in the driver's seat, started the engine and drove off.

I went back to the victim who had by now stood up.

"I'm Bobby Marcotte, the new driver here. What's your name?"

"I'm Grant Johnson. Thanks again for helping me. Big Al Chalmers was going to really do a number on me."

"Why were they so mad at you?"

"I complained to the crew chief that Big Al was slacking off and sabotaging the grinder. His actions were putting the rest of our crew at serious risk of injury. Big Al found out that I had ratted him out and he wanted to punish me."

"Did the crew chief have a go at Big Al?"

"No he didn't. Gerry is scared shitless of Big Al but he did mention to him that someone had made a complaint and told him to stop screwing with the equipment. Big Al learned that it was me so he was waiting for me in the parking lot after the plant closed."

"Who was the other guy with Big Al?"

"His name is Paul Godfrey. He doesn't work at the plant but he's Big Al's best buddy and roommate. He drives Big Al to and from work every day because Big Al got nailed for drunk driving a few months back."

"Are you okay to make it home on your own?"

"My car's here. I'll be fine. Thanks again Bobby. I was really lucky that you came along when you did. I hate to ask this, but could you keep this altercation with Big

Al to yourself. I don't want the other workers to know what happened."

"I won't tell anyone at the plant, Grant. I've only met a couple of the employees anyway. This is just my second day on the job and I don't want to get into any trouble for fighting in the parking lot."

CHAPTER 6 (Learning the Ropes)

As I drove home, it was becoming apparent that Buxton Manufacturing was not very well run.

After supper I phoned Uncle Don and brought him up to speed on my early adventures at the plant.

He decided to call the plant manager and suggest that Al Chalmers be terminated immediately for sabotaging the equipment. Uncle Don promised not to mention the fight but would say that I'd been the one to alert him to the problem.

New York was a right to work state so no notice had to be given to a fired employee and no reason for the termination needed to be provided.

On Wednesday I was given a tour of the factory by Brian Kirkwood. He explained how the kitty litter was manufactured and advised that on some of my non-delivery days,

I'd be assigned to the grinding room.

By the time I took the tour, the employees already knew that Big Al had been fired and informed Brian that they were one man short today.

Brian showed me the clay brick kilns which were not in use at the moment and perhaps wouldn't be fired up again until spring.

He didn't bother to show me the office and mentioned that he didn't get along with Doris Elmy, the office manager. I told him how rude she had been to me on Monday morning.

Brian took me back to the kitty litter room and left me there to assist the crew.

The standard face masks the employees normally used weren't adequate for this room because of the dust so proper masks were mandatory whenever the grinding machines were in use.

At lunch time another member of the crew informed me that the cafeteria was closed because of

Covid-19 which meant that most of the employees went home for lunch or brought their own and ate it outside.

I rarely ate lunch anyway but I got a Pepsi from the vending machine and joined the crew on a picnic bench. It seemed wise to fraternize with the other workers in order to learn as much as I could about the factory.

Most of the lunch talk was about Big Al. None of the workers had a good word to say about him and Grant didn't mention last evening's fight.

I learned that there were four grinding machines, each with a crew of four guys. Two of the crews had been laid off back in March when the Covid-19 lockdowns began and to date there hadn't been enough orders to recall either crew. The office staff comprised the three ladies I had seen on Monday plus one sales representative and the plant manager. Brian and Gordie were the only shipping room employees. I was the one and only driver. The clay brick division had eleven workers but they had all been laid off in early August when the orders stopped coming in.

I was asked a few questions about myself but managed to satisfy any curiosity by implying that I had been a truck driver for several years.

During the afternoon I continued to help out in the kitty litter room. Because of my strength, the crew positioned me to be the one lifting the full bags of kitty litter from the packaging conveyor to the wooden pallets.

It was hard physical labor but suited me because I was in essence being paid to work out.

Nevertheless, I was glad to hear the closing whistle at four-thirty.

CHAPTER 7 (Damsel Rescue)

I was a bit late getting away from the plant because Grant wanted to chat with me in the parking lot. I used the opportunity to pump information out of him about how the factory seemed to be coping with the pandemic.

"We're all worried about our jobs. The orders just aren't coming in and we're afraid that one of the remaining litter crews might be laid off soon."

"Do you have any idea why the orders are down?"

"The only salesman we've got is an old drunk and I'm sure that doesn't help things. The plant manager never bothers us unless it's to tell us that we're being laid off. I don't know what he really does. Most days he's not even on site. Other than that, I don't have a clue but I doubt if the Covid-19 situation has much to do with our reduced orders. Folks still need clumping cat litter."

Grant got in his car and drove off.

I was now alone in the parking lot.

Before I started the engine, I pulled my smart phone out of the glove box and searched the internet about cat litter. The search results were too confusing to be informative. I had hoped to learn whether cheap imported kitty litter was responsible for Buxton's decline in sales.

I had spent more time on my smart phone than I realized and it was now almost dark.

I pulled out of the lot and drove down the concession road toward Wellsville.

A car was pulled off on the shoulder and a woman was standing beside her vehicle and gesturing for me to stop.

I pulled off the road in front of her car and walked back to where she was standing.

"Are you having car trouble, miss?"

"My car just died and my phone seems to have done the same thing."

"My phone is working. Do you want me to call for a tow truck?"

"That would be great."

"Are you a member of Triple A?"

"No I'm not."

"I can call a towing service in Wellsville and wait here with you until the tow truck arrives."

"That's so kind of you."

I made the call and gave the man specific directions as to our location as well as providing him with my smart phone number. He indicated that a truck would be dispatched immediately.

It was getting cold so I suggested that we wait inside my car.

"I'm so sorry to be keeping you from your family, sir."

"You're not inconveniencing me at all. I live alone and just finished work at Buxton Manufacturing about half a mile north of here. By the way, I'm Bobby Marcotte. Do you live in Wellsville?"

"No, I'm from Alfred. I'm an attorney and just wrapped up a house call at a rural address a mile or so back."

"Do you work for a law firm?"

"I'm a sole practitioner."

"How long have you operated your law office?"

"I was called to the New York bar in July of last year and opened my practice that September after being unsuccessful in finding employment with any of the law firms in this area of New York State."

"Are you the only attorney in Alfred?"

"No. There are a few other lawyers in town."

"Is Alfred your home town?"

"It is. Nobody in their right mind would actually choose to live there otherwise. Is Wellsville your home town?"

"No. In fact I've only lived there for the past four days when

I secured the temporary position as a truck driver for the plant."

"Where did you live before that?"

"I was on the road as a long distance driver for a couple of years. My own home town is Syracuse."

We chatted for a few more minutes. The girl's name was Jennifer Griffiths and she lived at her parents' home near Alfred.

I asked her if she ran her legal office from the home but she replied that she rented a small office on the second floor of an old building in downtown Alfred.

Lights could be seen approaching from the south and the revolving blue light indicated that it was the tow truck.

When the driver arrived, Jennifer instructed him to take her vehicle to a repair shop in Alfred.

I was about to say goodbye when the driver advised that because of the Covid-19 restrictions, he was not authorized to carry any passengers.

"I'll drive you home, Jennifer. We can follow the tow truck and make sure your car arrives safely at the garage in Alfred."

"You're a lifesaver, Bobby. Thank you so much."

CHAPTER 8 (Busted)

It was only about twelve miles to Alfred and the tow truck driver dropped the car off at the repair shop Jennifer has designated which was closed for the night.

Jennifer had talked the entire time about her struggles in establishing her business. She was concerned that perhaps she had made a big mistake in returning to her home town to open her law practice.

She used my phone to call her parents who had been holding supper for her. She asked if there was room for a guest and then asked me to join her family for the meal.

I was pleased to do so.

Her parents lived less than a mile from the town and as we pulled into the driveway, Jennifer squealed with delight that her older brother must be visiting.

When we entered the home, I met her parents who appeared to be in their sixties or early seventies.

Jennifer explained how we had met and mentioned that I was a truck driver who worked at a factory near the spot where her car had broken down.

Jennifer had been wrapped up the entire time in a coat, scarf and hat. When she removed those items and took her coat off, I was slightly taken aback. Jennifer was quite gorgeous, tall with long medium brown hair and a lovely figure.

"Where's Barry? That's his car out front, isn't it?"

"He's downstairs in the den making a business call," her mother answered. She turned to me and said that Barry was also an attorney who worked for a law firm in Rochester.

We washed up and sat down for dinner.

Jennifer's mother yelled down for Barry to come upstairs and eat his supper.

A moment later a tall muscular chap emerged from the basement. As I stood up to shake his hand, Barry blurted out, "I've met you before. You were on the Syracuse University karate team and beat our top fighter in the tournament finals one year. I was on the University of Rochester squad. I thought your first name was Benton."

"Benton is my middle name. Robert is my given name and I'm going by Bobby while I'm in Wellsville."

"You didn't mention that you went to university," Jennifer interjected.

"It never came up."

"You're also a lawyer, aren't you?" Barry asked.

I blushed.

"What are you talking about, Barry?" his sister snapped. "Bobby is a truck driver."

"Well, that may be true, little sister but he used to be an attorney at CROSSWELL LLP in Rochester."

"Is that true?" Jennifer queried.

"It is. I'm a real man of mystery, I guess. I didn't enjoy the work hours or the actual legal work at CROSSWELL so I quit and drove a truck for the next two years."

"Do you have any other secrets?" Jennifer asked.

"I'm also a Certified Public Accountant but I didn't like that career either so I took a year off and travelled around North America before deciding that I'd give law school a try."

"That's such a colossal waste," Jennifer exclaimed. "Did you get disbarred or something?"

"I simply wanted a change of pace. In fact I've kept up my membership in both professions including completing all the required continuing education courses. At some point I may return to accountancy or law so wanted to keep my options open."

"What sort of law did you practice?" Jennifer inquired.

"I specialized in family law disputes."

"What didn't you like about that area of the law?" Jennifer's father asked.

"It was depressing enough listening to the marital woes of client after client but even more discouraging was the firm's expectation that we would stir up the animosity between the spouses in order to drag out the files and earn more money."

We all paused for a moment while the various bowls of food were passed around.

"What made you decide to take the job in Wellsville if it's only temporary?" Jennifer asked.

"That's a secret that I'd better keep for the time being."

"How long do you expect to work there?" she persisted.

"I'd be surprised if I'm still there at Christmas."

"Where will you go after that?"

"I have no idea. I guess I could say that I'm using the Wellsville experience to settle on whether I want to be an accountant, an attorney or something entirely different. You might be interested to learn that I was accepted at medical school in Buffalo in the late summer of 2018 but at the last minute decided that being a physician wouldn't suit my temperament."

"Why is that?" Mrs. Griffiths asked.

"Seeing dozens of patients every day and listening to their ailments struck me as a terrible way to earn a living. I turned down the spot and spent two years driving tractor trailers around the country."

"I take it that you never married," Mrs. Griffiths chimed in.

"One of my many idiosyncrasies is that I seem to have a bit of a commitment phobia. That has meant no long-term career so far which has satisfied me and also no marriages, engagements or even serious romantic relationships. In fact I haven't even had a date since I was an attorney. The life of a truck driver is anathema to a lasting romance."

"Don't you get lonely?" Jennifer inquired.

"I seem to enjoy my own company. I'm really a very deep thinker and utilize my solitude to ponder a whole myriad of issues. As a matter of fact driving a semi was more conducive to hashing over weighty matters than being a lawyer or an accountant was. I also worked for a stock broker's office for a year immediately after I obtained my Bachelor of Commerce degree from Syracuse University."

"What didn't you like about that job?" Barry asked.

"The pay was excellent but the actual work involved serious ethical choices that made me uncomfortable. The investment world is a very cut-throat business and it seemed that the lower the probity of the brokers, the more successful they were."

The concentration of interest on me was beginning to make me uncomfortable.

"That's enough about me. I'd like to know more about Barry and Jennifer's careers while I've got the opportunity just in case I decide to make law my final job after all."

My tactic worked like a charm and the rest of the evening was taken up with the family telling me about their lives.

Barry insisted on taking down my smart phone number because he wanted to keep in touch.

I thanked Mr. and Mrs. Griffiths for their fine hospitality and said goodbye to everyone shortly after nine o'clock.

Jennifer particularly impressed me. She was scrupulously honest and incredibly intelligent, not to mention extremely pretty.

In fact I almost asked her out on a date but decided that doing so might make her uncomfortable. She had only invited me for supper because I had rescued her after her car broke down.

It had been a very informative and enjoyable evening.

CHAPTER 9 (Kitty Litter Business)

On Thursday I was on the kitty litter assembly line again.

I tried to pry information out of the other members of the crew but none of them knew much about the business. To them it was only a paycheck.

At lunchtime I sat outside with Brian Kirkwood.

"Some of the guys are worried about their jobs, Brian. Have you got any thoughts on why Buxton Manufacturing is floundering?"

"I try to keep my nose out of other people's affairs."

"Do you have any idea why the only locations we deliver to are in this general area of the state?"

"Those matters are above my pay grade."

"I haven't met the sales representative or the plant manager yet. What are they like?"

"They don't bother with the shipping room as long as we make the deliveries."

"Doesn't the sales rep check the orders from time to time to make sure they're being filled properly?"

"No."

"I've only been working on the kitty litter assembly line for a day and a half but the plant manager didn't show his face while I was there. That surprised me."

"Nothing should surprise you around here, Bobby. It's best to keep your opinions to yourself."

It was apparent that Brian didn't want to talk about the factory so I dropped the subject.

In the afternoon I did learn a few pieces of pertinent information. Apparently the plant manager's parking space was empty much more often than it was occupied. Also, one of the guys snickered that he had seen the manager kissing Doris from the office and guessed that they were having an affair. The employee had noticed the loving couple about a year ago on a Saturday evening at a casino in Farmington which was in the Finger Lakes Region southeast of Rochester.

After work I stopped in at a pet store in Wellsville and asked the clerk why they didn't sell Buxton's Best Kitty Litter which was produced right here in town. She summoned the store owner who said that no one had ever approached them from the company.

That evening I phoned Uncle Don and advised him of the various issues I'd already discovered about the factory. He said that he'd never had any difficulty reaching Art Buchanan, the factory manager although he added that he always contacted Art using Art's personal cell number.

"Have you reached any conclusions yet about whether I should close up the factory?"

"No I haven't although about half of the employees are on temporary layoff at the moment. I've been studying the sales and overhead numbers for the past several years and I did notice that the volume of clay purchased from the strip mine near Alfred has increased significantly over the past five years."

"Why does that matter?"

"The actual sales of kitty litter and clay bricks have dropped slightly during that period which made me curious as to why the factory required substantially more raw material. Did your own company accountants mention that anomaly?"

"No they didn't."

"Did the plant start using new equipment in 2016 which might have required more clay in order to produce the kitty litter?"

"The factory uses the same equipment they've used since long before I bought the operation."

"As plant owner, perhaps you could contact the mine and have their people email directly to you copies of their sales invoices for the past six years. That should enable me to correlate the discrepancy. The guys on the kitty litter assembly line told me that the process of manufacturing and packaging the kitty litter hasn't changed at all over the past several years. I don't know if that's also the case with the clay brick production."

"I can do that for you, Benny. I'll send you the information as soon as I receive it."

After we ended the call, I thought to myself that possibly my extensive education was becoming useful.

CHAPTER 10 (Surprise Date)

On Friday I was pulled off the assembly line in order to drive the factory dump truck to the strip mine in Alfred. Normally the mine delivered the raw clay directly to the plant but its trucks were spoken for all day and Buxton Manufacturing needed a load of clay immediately.

This vehicle was old and quite temperamental. Brian admitted that it was rarely utilized but today was an emergency because the orders to be shipped out next week couldn't be filled without more raw clay.

While my truck was waiting to be loaded at the Alfred mine, I learned the mine's routine for filling the clay deliveries which information might be helpful in my analysis of why we were purchasing so much more clay than in the past.

I returned with the load and Brian assisted me in dumping the raw clay into the factory's receptacles.

In the evening I examined again the accounting records which Uncle Don had originally provided to me.

Just before nine o'clock my smart phone buzzed.

It was Jennifer Griffiths.

"Hello, Jennifer. It's so nice to hear from you. Did they repair your car okay?"

"Yes they did and the bill was very reasonable. I'm so glad that I had it towed to a repair garage I trusted. How have you been?"

"I actually drove through Alfred today. Our plant needed some clay from the Alfred mine. I would have stopped to see your office but we needed the material immediately back at the factory or the kitty litter assembly line would have had to shut down."

"It would have been nice to see you. By the way, thanks again for rescuing me the other night."

"I was thrilled to be useful. Please thank your parents again for a delightful supper. I really enjoyed myself."

"We found your comments about your many career moves fascinating. That's really the reason for my call. I was wondering if you'd like to join me for dinner tomorrow night. Some of the local restaurants have resumed indoor dining."

"I'd love the pleasure of your company, Jennifer. It's so kind of you to think of me. I haven't made any friends around here yet."

"What have you been up to this evening?"

"I've been studying up on how Buxton Manufacturing conducts its business."

"Why do you need to know that?"

"It has to do with my reason for being in Wellsville, but that's really all I should divulge. Tomorrow if you don't mind, I'd like to grill you a bit on what it's like to operate your own small town legal practice. You didn't get much chance to speak at the supper table on Wednesday. Everyone was focusing on me and my bizarre past."

"I look forward to discussing my law practice with you. Do you remember how to get to my parents' home?"

"I do. I've got an acute sense of direction. What time would you like me to show up?"

"It will be Hallowe'en Night so perhaps you should arrive before it gets dark. You can visit with my folks for a few minutes before we head out to a restaurant."

"I'll be there. It will give me an opportunity to wear one of my suits assuming they still fit. Thanks again for calling, Jennifer."

CHAPTER 11 (Pre-Date Chatter)

On Saturday morning I offered to cut the lawn for Mrs. Salisbury and she was thrilled because the grass had grown into a rather unruly mess and her deceased grandson had looked after the lawn maintenance before he died suddenly in August of a brain aneurism.

I spent two hours sprucing up the yard and my landlord was very grateful with the vast improvement in the appearance of her property.

Her lawn likely wouldn't need to be cut again until next spring.

In the afternoon I performed another good deed and drove Mrs. Salisbury to the grocery store and a pharmacy. I purchased some food for myself at the same time.

At the food store I almost purchased a bouquet of flowers for Jennifer but changed my mind at the last minute. It was possible that she had no romantic interest in me but simply wanted to be friends with another attorney.

Finally I showered and dressed in a black pinstripe suit. I was glad that I had brought two of my suits on this excursion to Wellsville.

Jennifer answered the front door and looked stunning. She was wearing a lovely black dress.

I blurted out "You look absolutely beautiful" as soon as I saw her.

She blushed and responded that I looked very successful and dapper myself.

Her parents seemed pleased to see me and we sat down in their living-room. I declined their offer of an alcoholic drink, answering that I never consumed alcohol when I was driving.

When asked what I had been up to today, I admitted that I had cut the lawn and taken my landlady to the grocery store.

"You sound almost too good to be true," Mrs. Griffiths commented.

"In fact I'm the black sheep of my family. My parents and siblings are overachievers and they're all disgusted that I turned into a permanent student."

"How did you afford all the tuition fees?" Jennifer inquired.

"I'm proud to say that I never accepted any assistance from my parents even though they're very wealthy. I resided at home during my four years as an undergrad at Syracuse University and my karate scholarship looked after all the tuition and textbook expenses. After that my working stints together with partial scholarships provided me with enough savings to cover tuition and living costs."

"Are you saddled with a lot of student loans?" Mr. Griffiths asked.

"I never had to borrow a nickel in student loans which is likely one of the reasons that I continued to drift around from one career to another. That perhaps proves that financial freedom is overrated."

"I was burdened with more than $70,000 in student loans when I finally finished law school," Jennifer replied. "Barry had amassed even more than I did but he's paid them all off by now. The main reason I'm still living at home is so I can reduce my student debt. I'm embarrassed to still be living in the same bedroom I had as a child even though I just turned twenty-eight."

"The old saying is true," I replied. "It's not what you earn that counts. It's what you spend. You're wise to be serious about keeping your expenses low."

We chatted with Jennifer's parents for another fifteen minutes at which point she announced that we'd better head over to the restaurant.

CHAPTER 12 (Fantastic First Date)

   We took my car to the restaurant Jennifer had suggested. In order to comply with the Covid-19 rules, we had to wear our face masks inside the establishment until such time as we were seated at our table.

   Jennifer ordered a glass of white wine and I requested a Pepsi.

   "One unusual thing that I noticed at your parents' place both on Wednesday and just now is that they didn't bring up politics or the pending election. The news is fixated on the race between Joe Biden and Donald Trump."

   "My family just isn't very political and they don't support either party exclusively. We all have a very negative opinion about politicians."

   "I've been following the election hype since I quit the

trucking job last month but before that I wasn't interested."

"Who do you hope wins next week's election?"

"I'm mildly rooting for Donald Trump because I felt he was doing a great job until the Covid-19 pandemic hit. The Democrats seem to favor defunding the police, opening the borders and allowing protest riots to continue."

"Where will you vote?"

"I won't be casting a vote. Presumably I'm on the rolls for Alexandria Bay but it's too far to drive there just to vote and I couldn't be bothered to request a mail-in ballot. My parents are at their winter home in Arizona right now."

The server returned with our drinks. We asked her to give us a few minutes before we placed our food order.

"You never asked me why I haven't married yet," Jennifer asked.

"You're quite gorgeous. I just assumed that you're a bit like me and haven't found the right guy yet. I'm sure the boys are hounding you for dates."

"That was true in Rochester when I attended university and then law school but Alfred is so small that virtually nobody returns here once they head off to college. By the time local guys are my age, they're married with three kids or already divorced. That's why I was so surprised when Barry said at the supper table that you had attended university."

"I'm close to unique, I guess. My family moans that I'm a classic underachiever."

"Somehow I'm positive that you were an excellent employee at all of your past jobs. Do you trust me enough yet to disclose your fascinating secret about why you're temporarily driving a truck for a small factory in Wellsville?"

"I am quickly warming up to you, Jennifer. If I tell you the real reason why I'm at Buxton Manufacturing, will you promise to keep the information to yourself for the time being?"

"I won't divulge your secret, Bobby."

"My Uncle Don owns the plant and it has been losing money lately. His accountants and lawyers have advised him to close the factory but he's reluctant to do that just before Christmas. I was in between jobs and we came up with the idea of me working at the plant in order to determine whether the business is viable and if so, what changes need to be made. The only opening was as the factory's truck driver and coincidentally I possessed the required commercial driver's licence."

"Have you reached any conclusions yet?"

"I'm still accumulating data."

"Does being the truck driver provide you with much opportunity to evaluate the business?"

"That's a very perceptive question. Actually it has allowed me to blend in as an ordinary Joe because I'm also working the production line when I'm not making deliveries. No one suspects that I'm anything but the new truck driver."

"How can you access the company's books if you're driving the truck or working on the assembly line?"

"My uncle is able to send me any data I request onto my laptop. He provided me with his accountants' summary and significant other data before I arrived in Wellsville and I'm waiting now for some additional information from him."

"Are you enjoying being an undercover snoop?"

"I am so far. My uncle hopes that I'll be successful in finding a way to save the company."

"Will you be able to do that?"

"It's too early to tell."

The server returned and we quickly made our choices and placed our food orders.

The remainder of the evening was fantastic.

Jennifer and I chatted in great depth about an assortment of issues, one of which was her legal practice and the types of files she was handling.

She preferred what she termed "happy law" and hoped eventually to specialize in real estate transactions, both residential and commercial. She only had a part-time secretary who normally worked on Thursdays and Fridays.

Jennifer had also accepted a few small claims court disputes in order to generate a bit of extra income but had avoided family law and criminal cases. She had prepared a few wills and expected to handle simple estate work but to date no estate files had come in.

Her largest file was an automobile accident case which she accepted on a contingency basis. The file seemed relatively minor when she agreed to act for the injured driver, but had since mushroomed into a complex mess. No settlement had yet been reached and the matter might actually be set down for trial in the near future, a prospect which terrified Jennifer. In fact she wished that she had never taken on the matter and had suffered through many sleepless nights because of it.

The evening flew by and the server announced that the restaurant closed at ten o'clock in compliance with the Covid-19 restrictions.

I paid the bill despite Jennifer's protestations and drove her back home.

"I've had a great time, Bobby."

"So have I. I'd love to take you out again but I won't put you on the spot right now. I'll call you early next week."

She smiled and replied that she looked forward to my phone call.

I walked her to the front door but didn't try to kiss Jennifer goodnight.

On the drive back to Wellsville I realized how much I had missed dating an attractive and intelligent girl.

CHAPTER 13 (Discrepancies)

Uncle Don had sent six years of clay invoices to my laptop but I was too tired to look them over.

On Sunday morning after breakfast I opened the laptop and began examining the documents Uncle Don had obtained and forwarded to me.

It would have been handy to have a printer available and after scrolling back and forth on the laptop too many times to count, I drove to an office equipment store and purchased a small printer and some paper.

That made my investigation immeasurably easier and I began to print off the invoices and sort them by date.

When that task was completed, I began listing the payments of those same invoices.

There were no discrepancies.

Every invoice had been duly paid and I printed off a copy of every payment check and stapled that check to the applicable invoice.

The company's accounting records corresponded precisely to both the invoices and payments.

The plant had been modestly profitable continuously from when Uncle Don purchased it in 2008 until 2015.

Since early 2016 however the business had been losing increasing amounts of money annually.

Although I only had Alfred Mine invoices from the beginning of 2015, I began studying them in more detail.

The overall purchase amounts of the clay had increased significantly in 2016 and had then remained relatively stable for each year from 2016 to and including 2020.

The anomaly which was confusing me was that the amount of product produced and shipped in each of those years was between five and fifteen percent less than in 2015 which didn't make a lot of sense since so much less clay was purchased in 2015. One possibility was that the factory had a large inventory of clay left over from 2014.

I checked the accounting records from 2013 and 2014 which revealed no stockpiled surplus clay.

I speculated that theoretically the manufacturing process had changed in 2016 in some manner not involving the equipment such that less kitty litter could be produced per truckload of clay. That possibility didn't correspond to the information I'd gathered from the work crew who told me that the process hadn't changed since any of them had begun working at the plant.

A different grade of clay was utilized in the brick production and those shipments of raw clay had remained stable over the past six years.

I re-sorted the invoices and payment checks by separating them into a kitty litter clay pile and a brick clay pile.

The brick clay purchases were uniform throughout so I put them aside and began focusing on the kitty litter pile.

This fiscal year 2020 was an anomaly because of the Covid-19 pandemic so I concentrated on comparing the profitable year 2015 with the four subsequent money-losing years including 2019.

Nothing seemed amiss with the invoices or the payments. The Alfred strip mine had sold us the precise quantities of kitty litter clay that we had subsequently paid for.

That was also true for 2020 up to the end of October.

Something wasn't adding up and I pondered over the matter until I got a headache.

No answer sprung to mind to explain the discrepancies.

CHAPTER 14 (An Inside Ally)

On Monday I made the various deliveries to Olean, Jamestown and Lackawanna and made it back to the plant at three-thirty.

On the drive back I'd had a mild epiphany regarding the clay deliveries and approached Brian Kirkwood as soon as I parked the truck.

"I've got another question for you, Brian. Last Friday when I drove the dump truck to Alfred to pick up the load of clay, I wondered whether you keep track of how much clay we receive."

"I do keep a record of the delivery dates and also whether it wasn't a full truck-load which doesn't happen often."

"The Alfred mine kept tabs of the clay they loaded into our own truck by weight. When the mine does the delivery directly to us, do they confirm to you the weight of the load?"

"No, but I can tell just by looking if we're getting a full load or if they're shorting us. They've never tried to shortchange us for the three years I've been working here."

"Is our dump truck the same size as the trucks from the mine?"

"Yes. In fact we purchased our old truck from the mine just after I joined the company. It was my own suggestion to protect us in the type of situation that cropped up on Friday when we needed clay immediately but the mine's only two trucks weren't available."

"Would you mind showing me the log you keep? The chap at the mine asked me to check how many loads they delivered here since October 1st. His records got wet and he couldn't read the numbers and his accounting office had asked him for the total. I forgot all about it until I was driving back to the plant after today's kitty litter run."

Brian was a trusting soul because he went to an old desk and brought out his log.

It was handwritten and not sophisticated at all but it did contain a record of the clay deliveries going back three years.

"Was keeping this log another one of your ideas, Brian? It only goes back for three years."

"Nobody else even knows about it. I began writing down the deliveries as soon as I started the job. It just seemed smart to keep track of the loads. You're not really a truck driver, are you?"

"Why do you say that?"

"You're too curious and the questions you ask are way too precise for what a driver would ever think of."

"You're very astute, Brian. I am a legitimate truck driver but I'm a lot of other things as well. Please keep that information to yourself for the time being. I'm going to borrow your log for the night but I'll bring it back to you tomorrow."

"Are you a cop?"

"No, but I am working undercover on behalf of the factory owner. The plant is losing money and I'm attempting to ascertain why that is. The owner doesn't want to close up this place unless he has no other choice so he sent me here to nose around."

"I was wracking my brain trying to figure out why you were asking me about the plant manager and the salesman. I also overheard you asking the guys on the crew a bunch of complicated questions. Now I know why."

"I may have more questions for you tomorrow morning before I do the east delivery run."

"I'll help you as best as I can."

CHAPTER 15 (Honing In)

I hid Brian's log under my sweatshirt as I left the factory at four-thirty.

After making a quick supper, I began comparing Brian's log entries with the invoices.

The evidence of fraud was clear.

The number of clay deliveries shown on the Alfred mine's invoices were more numerous than those shown on Brian's log.

It appeared that two truckloads each week were phantom orders in which the product was invoiced and paid for but never received. The average cost of a truckload of clay was $1,500 which meant that Buxton Manufacturing was paying each year for about $150,000 of clay it never received.

That amount meant the difference between the company losing about $125,000 each year or earning an income of $25,000 per year.

I phoned Uncle Don.

"I've pinpointed one major discrepancy already, Don. Someone is skimming about $150,000 out of your pocket each year by paying for clay deliveries that never arrive."

"That's disgusting. Who's involved?"

"It's too early to tell. The plant manager is certainly a prime suspect but he might have help from the office manager, Doris Elmy. Apparently they might also be romantically connected. There must be others involved as well. It could be someone from the Alfred mine but I've got no access to their accounting records. The payment checks from Buxton have all been deposited into the mine's bank account for every delivery including the phony ones."

"The owner of the mine is a close friend. I'll call her tomorrow and discuss the situation with her. She's no crook. I'd stake my life on it."

"Tuesday is one of my delivery days so I might not make it back to the factory by closing time but you can reach me at my apartment in the evening."

After I got off the phone with my uncle, I sat back and tried to unearth a way that someone from the Alfred mine could extract the phony delivery payment money from the mine's bank account.

No method came to mind unless the mine owner was involved and paid the other conspirators out of her own personal funds.

On Tuesday morning I told Brian that I needed to retain his log for another day or so. He had no problem with that and replied that until I returned it to him, he could keep track of the deliveries on a piece of paper and add the entries to the log later.

"Did you learn anything from looking over my delivery records?"

"Yes I did. Now I just have to pull on the thread a bit more to expose the whole scheme. Is my truck loaded up yet?"

"It's all ready for you."

The delivery run was quite tedious. Today was Election Day.

It took longer to unload the pallets of kitty litter because the recipients were short-staffed.

As a result I didn't make it back to Wellsville until quarter past five. I parked the truck in the lot and headed to my apartment.

Uncle Don called at six.

"I've spoken with Betty McDonald, the owner of the Alfred mine. She was shocked by what you told me and she wants to meet you tomorrow morning at nine o'clock to go over your evidence. Betty assures me that her accounting system is accurate with adequate fraud controls. She insists that the fraudsters must be at Buxton Manufacturing."

"I'll be at the mine office at nine o'clock sharp. With Betty's help and a bit of luck, hopefully we can figure out the rest of the scam."

After I ended the call, I phoned Brian Kirkwood at home.

"Hello Brian. This is Bobby. I won't be in to work tomorrow

morning. I've got an appointment in Alfred but I don't know how long it's going to take. It's even possible that I won't be in all day. I just wanted to let you know in advance."

Finally I called Jennifer and had a nice chat with her. I told her that I was going to be in Alfred tomorrow but didn't know if I'd have a chance to drop in and see her office.

We arranged to go out for dinner on Friday.

I was so busy poring over the accounting records that I went to bed without even knowing who had won the presidential election.

On Wednesday morning I was eating my breakfast while watching the news. Yesterday's election was an absolute farce. Half a dozen states were still too close to call and both sides were claiming election fraud by their opponents.

I left for Alfred and arrived at the mine a few minutes before nine o'clock.

Betty McDonald was a diminutive elderly lady with red hair, a great sense of humor and a foul mouth. I liked her from the moment we met.

"Don Adamson said that you were a man of many talents and even crazier than he is."

"That's true. I'm the number one black sheep of my family but Uncle Don runs a close second. Let's see if we can put our heads together and determine who has been cheating Buxton Manufacturing for the past few years."

We sat down in Betty's office and I showed her my evidence.

Betty called up her company's accounting records which showed the receipt of every payment including the phantom ones.

"That's one mystery solved," I said. "Your company has received every cent of the money we paid you. Are you positive that no one in the company could get their hands on the funds paid for the phantom deliveries?"

"I'm absolutely certain about that."

"In that case I don't understand how the fraudsters could profit from the phantom deliveries."

"If it wasn't the payment funds they were stealing, perhaps it was the shipments themselves," Betty surmised.

CHAPTER 16 (Bulls-eye)

I burst out laughing when Betty suggested that perhaps someone was absconding with hundreds of truckloads of raw clay.

"Don't you laugh at me, you pathetic little puke," Betty snapped.

"I'm sorry Betty but I can't fathom why someone would want tons of clay unless they're building a stairway to heaven."

This time Betty laughed out loud.

"Pure speculation won't get us anywhere. Let's take a closer look at the invoices and your shipping clerk's log book."

By comparing her shipping records with those of Buxton Manufacturing, we determined that both sets of records meshed perfectly.

Then we listed what we called the phantom deliveries, namely those that weren't recorded on

Brian Kirkwood's unofficial log book.

Betty got out a perpetual calendar and noticed that virtually all of the phantom deliveries had occurred on Fridays.

She picked up her phone and called her shipping manager.

"Hey Janie, this is Betty. I want you to round up the drivers' registers for the past six years and bring them to me right away."

While we waited, Betty asked me to explain why I'd driven a truck for the past two years when I was a qualified lawyer and accountant.

I related my negative impression of the work I'd done as a stock broker's assistant followed by my two years in an accountant's office and later as a family law attorney, but I could tell that Betty thought I was daft.

The shipping manager arrived with the driver records.

"Are these records accurate, Janie?"

"Yes they are ma'am. We're pretty anal about keeping track of which driver delivers which loads."

"How many drivers have we had in the five years shown on these records?"

"Jimmy Nelson has been with us for seven years and Jimmy's our main driver. It's unusual for us to keep a second driver for longer than a few months because we can't offer them enough hours to keep them with us."

"How many drivers normally work on Fridays?"

"Only Jimmy works Fridays. Most of our customers don't want to accept deliveries on Friday."

"We've got two trucks. How does Jimmy handle his Friday runs?"

"He takes the first load to the customer while we're filling the spare truck. When he returns after dumping his first load, he hops in the second truck and makes the delivery using it. We found that it saves time because it means that Jimmy isn't waiting around picking his nose while we fill the second truck."

"Thank you, Janie. I'll call you if I have any other questions. Please don't repeat our conversation to anyone."

Betty contemplated what we had learned for a moment.

"I think we've pinpointed which driver is hauling the phantom clay deliveries but we haven't determined where he's taking the loads."

"How will you figure that out?"

"I'll have someone I trust follow Jimmy on Friday and then I'll report back to you. I must admit that I'm highly embarrassed to learn that one of my employees may be in on this theft ring."

I thanked Betty for her assistance.

It was a few minutes past noon. I phoned Jennifer and said that the meeting lasted longer than I expected and that I felt that I should get back to work right away.

When she replied that she had been looking forward to seeing me, I asked her if she wanted to go out for supper this evening and she seemed very pleased to accept.

Back at Buxton Manufacturing, Brian asked how my appointment went and I responded that the mystery was gradually being solved.

He put me on the kitty litter assembly line for the rest of the afternoon.

CHAPTER 17 (Phantom Recipient)

After work I quickly showered and dressed in casual clothes for tonight's date with Jennifer.

We went to a different restaurant.

I didn't update Jennifer on my investigation other than to say that it was progressing satisfactorily.

She had a small claims court trial come up unexpectedly in the afternoon and told me all about it. Jennifer thought that she had presented her client's argument well but the judge had reserved her decision.

Again we were kicked out of the restaurant at ten o'clock but this time we shared a delicious and rather prolonged goodnight kiss.

I took that as a very positive development.

Thursday was uneventful. I worked the assembly line all day.

In the evening I had a chat with Uncle Don who had spoken with Betty last evening. We all hoped to discover the final piece of the puzzle tomorrow.

Jennifer phoned at eight o'clock and we spoke until after ten o'clock. She was so easy to talk to.

As earlier arranged, I phoned Betty McDonald at lunch time on Friday because Jimmy's deliveries were scheduled for Friday morning.

"I've discovered who is benefitting from the free clay," she cackled. "Can you meet me here at my office at two o'clock? I've arranged for Don to join us on speaker phone at which time we can decide how to handle what we've learned."

"I'll take the afternoon off and see you at two. I'm looking forward to finding out the gory details."

I told Brian that I felt ill and had to go home. He winked as he replied that he'd look after things in my absence.

To avoid driving back and forth from Wellsville to Alfred, I went home and put on a grey business suit which would do nicely for tonight's dinner date with Jennifer.

I arrived at the mine just after one-thirty and Betty led me into her office.

She called Don who was home and we began the meeting.

Betty took control.

"I think we've now got a handle on how the theft works. Our main driver Jimmy Nelson is definitely in on the scam. Our records show that he's supposed to deliver two truckloads of clay to Buxton Manufacturing every Friday. Your company records show that the clay is received and consequently Buxton remits payment to us."

"Does the clay actually exist or is it just a paper transaction?" Don asked.

"The clay is real. We load up one of our trucks and Jimmy delivers it. When he returns, our second truck is already loaded at which time he delivers that load of clay."

"If Buxton isn't getting the clay, then where is it going?"

"That's what we found out today when we followed Jimmy. Both loads were delivered to the Carlonte Tile Company in Hornell."

"Who are they?"

"I had to look them up on the internet. They're a small local manufacturer of various clay tiles."

I interjected with a question.

"Do you have any idea what Carlonte's connection is to Uncle Don's plant manager and office manager?"

"I don't but it shouldn't be too difficult to find out," Betty answered.

Don asked if we should be getting the police involved at this juncture.

"It might be wiser to have a corporate search done first on Carlonte Tile Company," I replied. "If the owner has deep pockets, then perhaps the matter could be resolved without criminal charges assuming that the stolen money is returned to your company."

"How much have they stolen from me in total?" Don inquired.

"The grand total is just shy of $750,000" I responded.

"Recovering those funds would enable me to keep Buxton Manufacturing open. Do you think anyone else might be involved?"

"That's not too likely. Jimmy Nelson probably just gets a small weekly kickback for redirecting the deliveries. Art Buchanan and Doris Elmy would certainly get a much bigger share of the profit but Carlonte Tile would be the main beneficiary. I doubt if they need any other co-conspirators."

"I'll call my lawyers right now and have them do the corporate search," Uncle Don said. "Once we know who the owners of the company are, then we can check property records to see what real estate assets the principals might have."

While we waited for Don to call us back, Betty and I got on the internet and attempted to find additional information about Carlonte Tile.

Their website indicated that the company had been in existence since 1973 but it didn't contain any personnel information. We did learn that the corporation was privately and locally owned.

Don phoned thirty minutes after we had ended the earlier call.

"The conspiracy veil has been pierced," he announced excitedly. "The company is owned 75% by Jerome Buchanan, 20% by Arthur Buchanan and 5% by Doris Elmy."

"That's fascinating," I blurted out. "Now let's see what information we can discover about the assets held by those three scoundrels."

Don thanked Betty for her very competent assistance and requested that she not fire Jimmy Nelson until Don and I had completed our investigation about the assets and relationship of the principals of the scam.

I also thanked Betty and left the mine office. It was just after four o'clock and I thought I'd drop in and see Jennifer's legal office.

She was still working when I arrived.

CHAPTER 18 (Raw Intelligence)

I met Jennifer's part-time secretary, a young lady named Brenda Hall. Her workday ended a few minutes after I arrived.

As soon as Brenda left, Jennifer kissed me hello and asked how my meeting went.

I was too excited to keep our progress secret and animatedly told Jennifer the stunning connections we had discovered earlier this afternoon.

Both of us jumped on the internet and began searching for personal information about the conspirators.

Jennifer was the first to make a breakthrough. She found a newspaper article in the Hornell newspaper from 2013 reporting that Carlonte Tile had been sold by the Carlonte family to another prominent local family and that Jerome Buchanan would run the enterprise.

Between my laptop and Jennifer's desktop office computer, we learned after a bit of digging that the Buchanan family owned several other businesses including a new car dealership.

The family was headed up by a matriarch named Edith Carlow Buchanan. Edith was from another wealthy local family and married Edward Buchanan in 1957. Edward had passed away in 1998.

Edith and Edward had two sons, Jerome and Arthur as well as an older daughter Belle.

Further searches indicated that Edith and Belle were astute businesswomen who ran most of the family's operations.

It appeared from some of the older newspaper articles that Jerome was a bit of a rogue and immersed himself in occasional scandals when he was younger.

The only article we found on Arthur Buchanan was a brief fluff piece in the local news section in the summer of 2006 mentioning that Arthur had taken a position as plant manager at Buxton Manufacturing in Wellsville.

It appeared that neither Arthur nor Jerome had ever married and in fact, both brothers had residence addresses in the Hornell area.

We looked up Doris Elmy. There was nothing about her on the internet but Jennifer did notice that there was a D. Elmy in the Hornell phone book. I checked the Buxton Manufacturing records and saw that the phone number shown on her employment application was the same as in the Hornell telephone book.

I called Uncle Don back from Jennifer's office and brought him up-to-date on our internet searches.

He had met Edith Carlow Buchanan twice in recent years at business conventions and decided that he would set up a meeting with her, himself and me as early as tomorrow if he could make the arrangements.

Twenty minutes later Uncle Don called me back on my smart phone.

We would meet Edith tomorrow at her mansion near Hornell at ten o'clock in the morning. Don asked me to bring all pertinent records proving the fraud, and he provided me with Edith's home address.

Since I had everything I needed in the trunk of my car, Don decided to book a hotel room in Hornell for tonight for the two of us in order to avoid having to drive to Hornell early tomorrow morning.

I said that I'd arrive at the Hornell hotel around eleven o'clock this evening after my dinner date.

Jennifer and I had a wonderful time at the restaurant and I sensed that we were growing very fond of each other very quickly.

We kissed much more passionately when I dropped her off at her house a few minutes after ten o'clock.

Then I drove the ten miles northeast to Hornell, New York.

CHAPTER 19 (Resolution)

Uncle Don was still up and dressed when I arrived at our shared room.

We pored over the evidence we had amassed and decided to hit the sack just before midnight.

On Saturday morning we woke early, ordered room service breakfast and discussed how we would approach Edith Carlow Buchanan.

Uncle Don appointed me to handle the encounter. He would simply introduce me as his nephew and let me describe in my own words how Buxton Manufacturing had been defrauded over the past five years.

We drove both cars to the home which turned out to be an impressive mansion just east of Hornell on the Canisteo River.

A butler greeted us at the front entrance and escorted us to an opulent study where a pot of coffee and pastries had been set up for us.

After the introductions were made, a maid served us coffee and departed.

I took a few sips of coffee while Uncle Don and our hostess made small talk about the election results and how they felt it would affect their various business operations.

Finally the conversation shifted when Mrs. Buchanan inquired as to the purpose of our visit.

"I'll let my nephew handle the explanation, Edith."

"Please let me start from the beginning, Mrs. Buchanan."

I proceeded to set out the chronology from Uncle Don's phone call looking for advice from my mother until I began working as the plant's truck driver just two weeks ago.

"My undercover assignment was merely to ascertain whether the company could be made viable because Don was very reluctant to close the factory permanently just before Christmas."

"Has Arthur not been managing the business properly?" she interrupted.

"That's an understatement, ma'am. I discovered from an examination of the company's accounting records that the factory was utilizing substantially more raw clay from the Alfred strip mine even though our orders and therefore our kitty litter production were down."

At that point I explained how the shipping manager had kept his own log of all raw material deliveries and that record differed significantly from the clay invoices from the strip mine.

"Uncle Don was a friend of the owner of the strip mine, Betty McDonald and she offered to peruse her records in order to ascertain why there was such a discrepancy. We discovered that every Friday for the past five years, the mine's delivery records corresponded with their invoices sent to Buxton Manufacturing."

"I'm not seeing any problem and in fact I'm wondering why you are bringing this matter to my attention."

"The problem is that on virtually every Friday for the past three years, two full loads of clay were supposed to be sent to Buxton according to the records of both companies, but the shipping manager's log revealed that those deliveries never arrived."

"Could the shipping manager's records be wrong?"

"On Friday Betty McDonald had someone follow the individual truck driver who had regularly made all of those Friday deliveries. The loads were dropped off at the Carlonte Tile Company here in Hornell."

Mrs. Buchanan sat back and appeared to be deep in thought for a full minute. Finally she told me to continue.

"It appears that your two sons, Arthur and Jerome, with the assistance of Buxton's office manager, Doris Elmy and a truck driver named Jimmy Nelson at the Alfred strip mine have conspired for the past five years to defraud Buxton Manufacturing. Even though the manager's log only goes back three years when the chap began working at Buxton, the company's lack of profit for the two prior years indicates that the theft has been ongoing for five full years. The thieves have in fact stolen approximately three quarters of a million dollars of clay from Buxton presumably to use in Jerome's tile business."

Mrs. Buchanan let out a huge sigh.

"I see. Are my sons aware of your recent discoveries?"

"No they're not, Mrs. Buchanan. When I reported my findings to Uncle Don yesterday afternoon, he suggested that we bring the issue to your attention first."

"If Buxton Manufacturing's losses are reimbursed immediately, will that resolve the matter fully?"

Uncle Don answered.

"That would satisfy me, Edith. Of course I'll have to terminate Arthur's employment as well as that of Doris Elmy but recapturing the losses from your sons' theft will allow me to continue operating the Buxton factory and as far as I'm concerned, everything will have been rectified. Obviously no one outside of the parties involved need be apprised of the true situation."

"I fully agree. With your permission I'd like to summon Arthur and Jerome here now along with Ms. Elmy who currently resides with Arthur. Are you willing to wait here so that Mr. Marcotte can personally bring them up to speed about his unsavory discoveries?"

"We're at your disposal, Edith. It would please us greatly to put the whole matter to rest once and for all today."

Mrs. Buchanan made the two phone calls and thereafter informed us that the three co-conspirators would arrive within ten minutes.

The full meeting was relatively short and somewhat anticlimactic.

Jerome and Arthur seemed to be genuinely humiliated that their scam had been uncovered. Doris Elmy was too inscrutable to read.

They admitted everything. Jimmy Nelson was only paid thirty bucks per illicit truckload. The kid was now going to lose his full-time job over what amounted to an under-the-table stipend of about $3,000 per year.

We confiscated their keys to the factory and obtained their computer passwords.

Edith Buchanan called her banker even though it was now early Saturday afternoon and she wired the sum of $750,000 into the business account of Buxton Manufacturing.

Uncle Don and I left the mansion and he asked if I'd mind meeting him at the factory as soon as we arrived in Wellsville. I drove behind him all the way and we reached the plant about forty minutes after we'd started out.

CHAPTER 20 (Driver and Manager)

When we got to the factory, Uncle Don used the keys he had confiscated from Arthur and Doris to enter the building.

"You've done a stellar job of evaluating this operation, Benny. On the drive over here I was mulling over what comes next with Buxton Manufacturing."

"What are your options?"

"I could still close it down. Even with the capital infusion from Edith Buchanan, the plant has really only broken even for the past five years."

"Since the staff still working at the factory has now been reduced to thirteen including me, it would be a logical time to shut the plant. What are your other choices?"

"The only other possibility that comes to mind is to continue to operate the business as a going concern while I find a buyer for it. I'm most embarrassed to have discovered through you that the plant manager and office manager have been stealing from me. I trusted them. Both Art Buchanan and Doris Elmy held those managerial positions when I bought the business from the Buxton family. They told me that both managers were top-notch. I have learned a valuable lesson, however."

"What lesson is that?"

"There's no point owning a business unless I can exercise some hands-on control of the operation. I've got a couple of other small factories that I've also been neglecting. Relying on the plant managers together with my accountants and lawyers to maintain profitability and also spot discrepancies clearly didn't work in the Buxton instance."

"Will you take over the management of Buxton Manufacturing for the time being?"

"I know nothing about the kitty litter business or the clay brick division at this factory, but I need someone I can trust implicitly. That's where you come in."

"I don't follow you."

"I'd like you to manage the plant over the winter and see if you can improve its profitability. In the spring I'll either close the plant or try to sell the business. Will you do that for me?"

"Will I have authority to make any changes I deem necessary?"

"I'll give you total control over the plant because I trust you and because I've known for many years that you're by far the smartest person in our entire family."

"I accept, Uncle Don. If nothing else it will expand my résumé but I'm also hoping that I can turn the business around. Perhaps you'll even decide not to sell it."

"In that case I'm going to book a hotel here in town for a few nights. How do you want me to handle the transition of management over to you?"

"I'd prefer to be just the truck driver for the delivery runs on Monday and Tuesday. Perhaps you could inform the staff on Monday morning about the departure of Art Buchanan and Doris Elmy and also let them know that you'll introduce the new plant manager at a special meeting first thing on Wednesday morning. There's one other matter I'd appreciate your assistance with."

"What's that?"

"The rumor among the workers is that the sales representative is a drunk who doesn't really do anything worthwhile. Perhaps we could check out his sales call log if we can locate it and verify whether he actually made the calls he claims. I discovered that the local pet stores don't even stock our brand of kitty litter and I suspect that the rumors are correct about our one and only salesman."

"Do you want me to sack him if we confirm that he's been falsifying his work log?"

"That would be helpful. I don't want to get on the bad side of the employees on day one."

"Surely you don't intend to operate as both the truck driver and the plant manager."

"I just might do that. Apparently Art Buchanan's vehicle was absent from his parking spot more often than it was on site. Continuing as the delivery driver two days a week will allow me to learn the nitty gritty of the kitty litter business from the ground up. In the dual role I can speak to our customers directly at their work places and perhaps make some needed changes."

"You're the new boss, Benny. I'll leave those decisions completely up to you."

"I suspect that as an accountant I might even be able to handle three positions without breaking a sweat. This afternoon and tomorrow I'd like to sit down with you and pore over the office records. My guess is that Doris Elmy didn't do much around here other than ensure that the invoices to the strip mine were paid promptly."

CHAPTER 21 (More Deadwood)

Uncle Don and I began searching through the office records.

That was illuminating.

Art Buchanan and Doris Elmy had provided us with their computer passwords in addition to their keys.

It didn't take me long to assess the information on their computers and learn the payroll system.

Buchanan's salary had been $190,000 annually and Doris Elmy earned $59,000.

The sales representative made a flat salary of $39,000 with no commission component. That likely explained why he had no incentive to locate new customers.

Brian Kirkwood only earned $25 an hour as shipping manager and his assistant's wages were $15 an hour. The two office clerks as well as the assembly line crew were paid between $15 and $17 an hour.

Uncle Don wanted to pay me what Art Buchanan had been earning but I argued that I'd only be working three days a week as the plant manager. We settled on a salary of $149,000 which I felt was all I'd be worth at least at the beginning until I learned a lot more about the kitty litter and clay brick businesses.

At five o'clock we called it a successful day and I went home to get ready for my date with Jennifer tonight.

Rather than go out for supper, she had invited me to her parents' home for the evening meal after which we would play cards with her folks.

I had a tremendous evening. After our card game, Jennifer's parents went to bed so I had an opportunity to apprise her of my most interesting day.

She seemed excited for me and gushed that my new position at the plant meant that I'd be sticking around the area longer than I had earlier anticipated.

"I really like small town living, Jennifer. There's a good chance that I'll make this area my permanent home."

"That's music to my ears, Bobby."

I didn't leave her house until almost midnight. It was evident that we were fast developing a serious romance.

On Sunday morning I met Uncle Don at the factory.

We managed to access the sales representative's office computer which wasn't even password protected. A search of his office uncovered several bottles of whiskey hidden in various ingenious locations.

Most of the recent searches on his computer had been porn sites which spoke volumes about how he passed his time while sitting in his private office.

We found the sales log from October on Doris Elmy's computer and within a few phone calls to the businesses shown on his log book we had confirmed that he hadn't contacted those enterprises in months.

The payroll records indicated that the sales rep had used up all his 2020 vacation and sick time already, and he had been paid on Friday for the period up to and including Friday.

Uncle Don called the fellow and sacked him over the phone. In a pathetic confirmation of the chap's priorities, he asked if he could come to the factory immediately and collect his personal effects which really meant his unused booze. Don told him to come right over but to bring all his keys to the factory.

The gentleman arrived fifteen minutes later with a cardboard box into which he packed his precious whiskey as well as a couple of photographs and some personal items.

To the man's credit, he admitted that he had an alcohol problem and apologized to Uncle Don for slacking off in recent years. He advised that he had turned sixty-two a couple of months earlier and had already applied to start collecting his social security pension.

He accepted our written termination notice and signed an acknowledgement that he had no further claims against Buxton Manufacturing Company and that he had been fully paid for all time worked up to date.

When the salesman left, Uncle Don queried whether there was any more deadwood in the factory.

I responded that the kitty litter crew and shipping room workers appeared to be reliable employees now that the bullying troublemaker had been terminated two weeks earlier.

CHAPTER 22 (Unusual Announcement)

I drove the transport on Monday and Tuesday and managed to make arrangements with the recipients of the deliveries that in the future we would deliver double the product every second week. I had noticed since beginning employment as the driver that the semi was less than half full which made no economic sense.

The recipients were actually middle-men which then distributed our product to the individual stores in their sales area.

Brian Kirkwood informed me on Monday afternoon when I returned from the delivery run that the plant manager, office manager and sales rep had all been terminated and that the company owner was running the business for the time being.

"Were you already aware of those changes?" he inquired.

"Actually I was. There will be a full staff meeting regarding the new plant manager on Wednesday morning, but keep that information to yourself until the owner announces it."

I did inform Brian of the new bi-weekly shipping schedule. He confirmed that there was enough finished product on hand to make the double-sized deliveries next Monday and Tuesday.

Jennifer and I had long conversations on the telephone each night and I told her about all the changes as they occurred.

On Wednesday morning I arrived for work in my black pin-striped business suit.

Every remaining employee assembled at the factory office at eight-thirty when the business opened.

Uncle Don addressed the group.

"I'm Donald Adamson, the owner of Buxton Manufacturing Company. You've probably noticed some major changes around here earlier this week. The plant manager, the office manager and the sales representative are no longer employed by the company. My nephew, Robert Benton Marcotte will be taking over the management of the business effective immediately. I'll let Mr. Marcotte introduce himself."

I had been out of view in my new office.

When Uncle Don uttered that sentence, I emerged from the office to a cacophony of gasps. No one around here had ever seen me in a suit and tie.

"Good morning everyone. Most of you already know me as Bobby, the company's new truck driver. I am a certified driver with a valid commercial licence and was employed as a long distance trucker for the past two years, and I intend for the time being to continue making the deliveries until a new driver is hired."

The room was incredibly silent.

"In fact I'm a man of many talents. I hold my Certified Public Accountant designation for the state of New York and I'm also a qualified attorney with the New York State legal bar. For at least the next few months I'm going to add to my résumé significantly as I take over the combined positions of plant manager and office manager."

The employees seemed stunned by my qualifications.

"I suppose the question on everyone's lips right now is why I've been driving the company delivery truck. I've been what you might term an undercover trucker since I began work here. My uncle and I felt that I could learn more about the business and why it was floundering if I was an ordinary employee than I could have discovered by joining the office staff."

Gordie, the shipping department assistant, raised his hand as if I were his teacher.

"Yes, Gordie, what do you want to know?"

"If you're a lawyer, why are you still going to drive the delivery truck?"

"There are two reasons. First off, I enjoy driving a big rig, but the main reason is that Buxton Manufacturing needs a driver. It's crucial to getting our product delivered to our customers. At some point very soon I expect that we'll hire a regular driver but for now I'm happy to carry on as the plant's driver. Being alone on the highway gives me plenty of time to dream up ways to make your lives miserable around here."

My joke was met with slightly nervous laughter. After all, no one had any inkling of what I would be like as the big boss.

"By the way, I'm very receptive to suggestions of ways to make our product and service better. Please don't be shy about running your ideas by me. Now please get back to work. Together we can make this place profitable again."

Uncle Don decided to drive back to Rochester but he mentioned that he was going to phone Betty McDonald and hopefully take her out to lunch in order to thank her in person for helping us solve the mystery of the missing clay.

CHAPTER 23 (New Hires)

On Thursday I began inquiries about locating a gung-ho sales representative and contacted three potential candidates whose names had been supplied to me by our employees.

I preferred not to advertise the position because of the possibility of human rights or other discrimination claims from disgruntled applicants who were not selected.

One woman in particular seemed to be an excellent choice. Her children were grown up and she had resided in Wellsville for the past twenty years, previously having lived and worked in Bath and Elmira doing various sales jobs.

Her name was Grace Neufeld and she had been furloughed since April at the restaurant supply company where she had worked in the sales division for the past four years.

I interviewed Grace and learned that her husband was a local home renovator and that Grace and her spouse were avid animal lovers.

She agreed to commence employment with Buxton Manufacturing immediately and we settled on a compensation package with a base salary of $30,000 annually plus a commission on any orders from new customers and on any increased orders from our existing clients.

As far as a new truck driver was concerned, Brian Kirkwood provided the name of a friend of his who had been a long distance trucker for thirty-five years until he retired last Christmas.

The gentleman, whose name was Russell Morgan, had moaned to Brian that he was finding full retirement a bit boring and had been considering looking for a part-time job.

I spoke with Russell on the phone and he indicated that taking over the bi-weekly delivery runs would suit him perfectly for the time being.

Even more positive, Russell advised that he would also be available to make local deliveries if our new sales representative began locating additional customers for our kitty litter product.

Russell was satisfied with a wage of $22 an hour.

I recalled one member of a laid-off assembly line crew to fill in permanently for Big Al Chalmers, the idiot who had sabotaged the line and then picked a fight with Grant Johnson.

One pleasant surprise in the office was that Marcie Bateman had been posting the entries in our accounting records for several years and admitted that Doris Elmy had done very little actual work as office manager.

That meant that Marcie didn't require very much supervision or training.

Marcie's assistant was less efficient but did know how to complete the payroll each week.

By the time Friday closing time rolled around, I was confident that Buxton Manufacturing had a pretty decent team in place to maintain and even grow the business.

CHAPTER 24 (Finally Romance)

Jennifer and I had been chatting on the phone each evening and finally we were going to see each other on Friday.

She had shown an interest in seeing my apartment and the Buxton Manufacturing plant where I worked so we tentatively arranged that she would leave work early on Friday, drive directly to the factory where I would give her a quick tour and then Jennifer would stay overnight at my place after we had shared supper at a nice local restaurant.

It was a major step forward in our budding relationship but one that we had discussed thoroughly on the phone and felt comfortable with.

We enjoyed the restaurant in Wellsville and returned to my apartment just before ten o'clock.

For the next hour or so we sipped coffee in between brief sessions of cuddling and kissing.

Both of us were quite nervous when we decided that it was time to adjourn to the bedroom.

"What was your parents' reaction when you told them that you'd be staying over at my place tonight?"

"They seemed fine with it. Mom and Dad both like you a lot, Bobby."

"I'm relieved to hear that."

It was apparent that neither of us were experts at sleepover dates. We tentatively climbed into the bed while wearing our pajamas.

Eventually we stopped chatting and began kissing.

Inevitably as our passion fired up, our cloth defenses were removed and we began making love.

It was quite heavenly and shortly after we had consummated our relationship, Jennifer whispered that she had already fallen in love with me.

I replied that I was also in love with her.

Without explicitly expressing our thoughts about our future together, I felt that Jennifer and I would stay together forever and I was pretty confident that she felt the same.

The next morning when we woke up, there was no sign of remorse or embarrassment.

We had successfully taken our union to the next level.

After we'd showered and dressed, we decided to go out for breakfast.

At the diner Jennifer raised the issue of our current living arrangements.

"I loved sleeping with you, Bobby despite the rather downscale locale. How long do you intend to keep that dingy apartment?"

"It filled my temporary needs inexpensively while I was working in Wellsville but I've got to admit that connecting with you so wonderfully has made the apartment unsuitable. Uncle Don would like to sell the factory at which point

I intend to quit my position and set up my own legal office."

"Where will you do that?"

"My top priority is to please you, Jennifer. Alfred seems to be by far the best town to accomplish that goal. Perhaps we could even form a business partnership."

"I absolutely adore that idea, Bobby."

"In that case, rather than commit to an apartment lease, it might make sense for me to continue renting the existing apartment until the plant is sold. Then we can decide whether to rent or buy in Alfred."

Jennifer reached over and held my hand.

"That's music to my ears, darling."

In the afternoon we took Jennifer's car to Alfred. She had a client to see in her office and I used her secretary's computer to check out home prices in and around Alfred.

After a short visit at her parents' house, we drove back to

Wellsville and had supper at a different restaurant.

Jennifer stayed over at my place again.

On Sunday morning I gushed that it had been the best weekend of my life.

Since Jennifer had an early Monday morning appointment at her office, she drove back to Alfred on Sunday after we had eaten take-out Chinese food at my apartment.

CHAPTER 25 (Factory Sale Prospect)

On Sunday evening after Jennifer had left, I called Uncle Don and brought him up-to-date on the changes I had made at the factory over the past week.

He admitted that he was anxious to sell the business.

"I see from the accounting books that you rent the premises from the Buxton family," I mentioned.

"That's right. At the time I bought the business in 2008, I wasn't interested in purchasing the land and buildings."

"Do you have a written lease?"

"Yes but I've got my original copy here at my house."

"When does the term expire?"

"Hang on for a minute and I'll pull it out."

A few moments later Uncle Don came back on the line and informed me that the lease was for a fifteen year term and that it would expire on April 30th, 2023.

"That might make it tricky for any potential buyer," I mentioned. "The Buxton family night not be willing to renew the lease at all or would agree to do so only with a sharp increase in the rent."

"That's a good point, Benny. To encourage me to purchase the business, the rent was fixed at the bargain rate of $4,000 per month for the entire fifteen year term. Can you contact the Buxton family on my behalf and discuss the matter with them?"

"Send a copy of the lease to my office computer at the factory. I'll examine it tomorrow morning and call your landlord. If they don't want to renew the lease at all or if the rent they want is too high, then your options might be severely restricted."

"I agree. I'd rather just close the plant down as opposed to moving its location. Finding a properly zoned alternate site for what constitutes a rather dirty industry would be most difficult. Also, the very modest profit generated at the factory wouldn't justify renewing the lease at a much higher rent."

On Monday morning I read over the terms of the factory lease thoroughly.

Then I phoned Jane Buxton, the widow of the gentleman who had owned and operated the plant for more than three decades.

I introduced myself and decided to be completely candid with her.

"I'm managing the plant temporarily on behalf of my uncle who intends to sell the business or simply close it down. The issue of the existing lease came up last night and we realized that your input was crucial to Uncle Don's ultimate decision. The factory lease expires in two and a half years. No potential purchaser will likely buy the business without being assured that the lease can be extended and at an acceptable monthly rent."

"Wellsville is a small town, Mr. Marcotte. I'm aware that many of the current employees of the plant have been laid off and I've also heard through the grapevine that the business has been losing money for the past few years."

"That's correct, Mrs. Buxton. We discovered recently that the sales representative at Buxton Manufacturing was merely occupying his desk and had long ago stopped actively trying to market our products. He was terminated and the lady we hired as the replacement has already shown herself to be a vast improvement. We fully expect our orders to increase rather quickly in which case we'll be able to recall the laid off employees."

"I'm pleased to hear that. What about the profitability issue?"

"In fact that has been fully addressed. Strictly between us, we discovered that significant employee theft had been occurring since 2016. That leakage has been stopped and fortunately we managed to get reimbursed for the full estimated value of the company's losses since the thefts first began. As a result, the business has returned to profitability. Without the theft issue, the factory would have been modestly profitable every year despite the lack of an effective sales force."

"That's even better news. Would it be possible for me and my representatives to meet with you and Donald Adamson in the near future? My family might be interested in buying the business back from your uncle."

"That arrangement might be perfect for everybody concerned, Mrs. Buxton. Please advise me of a tentative day and time and I'll check with Uncle Don to ascertain whether he can accommodate you."

"I'll check with my people and get back to you later today."

In fact Mrs. Buxton contacted me a couple of hours later and suggested tomorrow at two o'clock in the afternoon. I called Uncle Don who said that the meeting was convenient for him.

One condition of the meeting, which was acceptable to my uncle, was that the Buxton family accountants would have complete access to our accounting records tomorrow before the meeting took place.

CHAPTER 26 (Satisfactory Negotiations)

I received a phone call just before closing time from the Buxton family accountant who was pleased to learn that I was a CPA.

We discussed what materials she required me to produce for tomorrow's afternoon meeting and we agreed to meet here at the factory at nine o'clock in order to examine the finances of Buxton Manufacturing Company thoroughly so that she would be fully conversant with the fiscal health of the business by the time the main parties met at two o'clock.

Jennifer drove to Wellsville after work and we ate supper at a family diner before returning to my apartment.

I told her about the promising developments at the factory and she stayed overnight.

On Tuesday morning Jennifer returned to Alfred and I went to the factory.

The accountant showed up right on time at nine o'clock. Her name was Marion Wishart and she was a pleasant lady who looked to be in her mid-sixties.

We examined in gory detail the accounting records right back to when Uncle Don had purchased the business in 2008.

"Why do you think the manager was able to cook the books since the beginning of 2016 without being detected?" she queried.

"My uncle was an absentee owner and relied too heavily on his staff."

"How did he finally spot the discrepancies?"

I explained in detail about the mystery of the excess clay being used in the manufacturing process and how the theft might not even have been spotted had it not been for the shipping manager's personal log book.

Marion was fascinated with how Betty McDonald and I had put our heads together to solve the paradox.

We continued to work right through the lunch period.

Uncle Don showed up at one o'clock and he answered some additional questions from Marion about the business.

By the time the other meeting participants arrived for the two o'clock meeting, Marion was confident that she had a firm handle on the financial health of the business.

Jane Buxton was an elderly lady in her early eighties but sharp as a tack.

Her grandson, Charles Buxton had recently obtained his MBA from State University of New York at the Rochester campus and Grannie was considering purchasing back her former business so that Charles could begin his career as the new manager of Buxton Manufacturing Company.

Marion summarized her findings about the company's finances and then Jane and Uncle Don went into my private office and hammered out the terms of an agreement.

They emerged an hour later having sealed the deal.

The closing date was set for December 1st but Charles would shadow me beginning tomorrow in order to learn about the kitty litter end of the business.

My own employment would terminate on December 1st.

Uncle Don and I had supper together.

"Benny, I can't thank you enough for what you've managed to accomplish in the past three weeks. You're a real whiz-kid just like I've always known you were. What are your plans now?"

"This temporary gig at your factory has worked out well for me also. I met a fantastic lady and we've fallen in love. Jennifer is an attorney in Alfred. I'm going to join her law practice and we'll probably purchase a home together

in the very near future. She still
lives at her parents' house while
she's been building her legal
business."

After supper Uncle Don drove
back to Rochester.

I phoned Jennifer and told her
the great news. She was so excited
that she drove to Wellsville and
brought a bottle of champagne
which we polished off up in my
apartment.

We discussed our future plans
and decided that I should give
Gertrude Salisbury notice that I'd
vacate this apartment on or before
Saturday, the 5th of December.

We were literally bursting with
happiness.

CHAPTER 27 (More Great News)

On Wednesday morning I began showing Charles Buxton the inner workings of Buxton Manufacturing.

He was a few years younger than me and demonstrated no spirit of adventure.

I couldn't discern any semblance of a sense of humor and I joked to Jennifer that Charles was the epitome of what most folks would term stuffy.

Even his manner of talking was stilted and oozed an air of haughtiness.

Nevertheless, he was clever and seemed to pick up the nuts and bolts of managing the factory quickly enough.

Since he demonstrated no curiosity whatsoever about me, he never learned that I was both an accountant and an attorney. The chap hadn't asked me a single personal question during our first week working together.

Any attempt I made to worm a bit of information about his personal life crashed and burned. Charles was inscrutable to the point of being almost robotic.

Since he had no personality, I began to dread each working day with Charles stuck to my ass like an unwanted hemorrhoid.

I moaned to Jennifer on the phone during the evenings while she remained in Alfred. Jennifer had a motor vehicle court case on the go this week in the village of Belmont which was the county seat of Allegany County. She worked late in her office each evening in order to prepare for the next day's trial witnesses.

On Saturday and Sunday we had supper together in Alfred after which I drove back to Wellsville.

A bit of great news greeted me on Monday morning. Our truck driver was ill and Brian Kirkwood had taken the week off as vacation time.

That provided me with an escape from boring Charles. I asked Mr.

Robot if he wanted to accompany me on the delivery run to learn that end of the business but his face scrunched up in distaste and he declined my offer.

The day behind the wheel of the semi was by far the best time I'd had since Charles was foisted on me.

Jennifer's court case was dragging on and in fact didn't end until Friday afternoon.

The judge had reserved her decision and Jennifer was frantic worrying about whether she had somehow butchered the trial.

I assured her that from what she described to me, she had done a tremendous job.

Jennifer and I went out for dinner on Friday evening in Wellsville. It was great to have her undivided attention again.

On Saturday morning we had just finished making our own breakfast in the apartment when Jennifer's smart phone buzzed.

It was the opposing attorney who represented the insurance company on the motor vehicle accident trial.

The company presented a much better settlement offer. Jennifer and I discussed the offer and we both felt that it was fair to the point of being generous.

She contacted her client who accepted the offer.

Jennifer called the other attorney back and arrangements were made to have the Minutes of Settlement prepared and signed immediately.

We drove together to Belmont to pick up the documents which had already been signed by the insurance company. We took those documents to Jennifer's client in Alfred, had the woman sign the papers and immediately delivered them back to the Belmont attorney.

Jennifer was beside herself with excitement and relief. She no longer had to worry about a judge's ruling in favor of the defendant insurance company's client, not to mention that Jennifer's contingency fee of thirty-three percent of the award meant that she had earned a whopping legal fee of $170,000.

Jennifer had paid out $24,000 in disbursements on the file, most of which had been paid using her business line of credit, but after she retired that line of credit, Jennifer would still be left with $146,000 before income taxes.

It would take a few days for the funds to arrive from the insurance company but that nightmare file was now finally put out to pasture.

We were too exhausted to dine out so we brought take-out food up to my apartment where we celebrated Jennifer's victory.

CHAPTER 28 (End of the Line)

Jennifer drove back to Alfred on Sunday morning so that she could spend the day preparing her final report on the insurance lawsuit file.

I spent the day doing various errands.

The ensuing week dragged a bit early on because I was stuck with Charles. Fortunately Thursday was a holiday.

Jennifer had been busy in Alfred working long hours so we spoke by phone in the evenings but didn't get together in person until Thanksgiving Day on Thursday when we ate supper at her parents' home before I drove back to Wellsville.

Her insurance check had arrived the previous day and Jennifer had proudly paid off her entire student loan balance as well as her business line of credit loan.

On Friday I was spared the company of Charles who had decided to take the day off.

Jennifer and I spent the weekend together in Wellsville. We relaxed and delved into each other's finances.

I had substantially more cash assets than Jennifer but now neither of us had any debts.

We perused homes for sale in the Alfred area but realized that the pickings were mighty slim at this time of year.

On Monday the 30th of November I said goodbye to the employees at Buxton Manufacturing since tomorrow was the scheduled closing date of the sale of the business back to the Buxton family and I expected to remain at the plant only for a few hours until the sale was officially completed.

December 1st arrived and Uncle Don drove down from Rochester for the turnover.

The sale closed without any glitches in the morning and I said goodbye to Charles Buxton and wished him all the best in his management of the business.

My days as an undercover trucker were over.

Uncle Don took me out for lunch.

"I'm thrilled to have that factory out of my care and control," he admitted. "It's a miracle that everything worked out so perfectly and I've got you to thank for that. I seriously doubt that anyone else could have solved the mystery of the missing clay."

"You may be correct. It was only my insertion as the truck driver that enabled me to learn the ropes quickly and ferret out the existence of the secret shipping log."

"I'm glad that you suggested that I toss Brian Kirkwood a bonus of $5,000 for his invaluable assistance in allowing the thefts to be uncovered."

"Brian was absolutely ecstatic when I handed him the bonus check yesterday," I replied.

"Speaking of thoroughly earned bonuses, I brought along a check for you as well. Your initial role as the undercover truck driver combined with your subsequent management of the plant was astounding. Do you still intend to join your girlfriend's law practice?"

"I do. Jennifer just settled a lucrative motor vehicle accident case and earned a tidy windfall for her efforts. We're going to buy a home together once the right property comes up for sale."

"In that case this bonus check should come in quite handy."

Don handed me the check and my jaw dropped.

I had already received my regular salary yesterday to compensate me for my time as manager and when I glanced at Uncle Don's check, my jaw gaped open.

It was in the amount of $50,000.

"This is so incredibly generous, Uncle Don."

"You earned every cent of it, Benny."

He changed the subject and we spoke about my parents. I'd been remiss and hadn't called them even once since shortly after I moved to Wellsville. Their disdain about my new trucking job had angered me.

My life was my own to live as I damn well pleased.

Uncle Don had called my folks on Thanksgiving Day and had assured them that he had been in regular contact with me and that I was doing just fine. He didn't mention that I'd been working at his factory because he wanted me to apprise my mother about my latest employment position.

Partly at Uncle Don's urging before we said our goodbyes, I phoned my parents from the restaurant parking lot.

Mom was surprisingly pleased when she learned that my latest truck driver position was at Uncle Don's factory in order to investigate whether the business could be salvaged. She was even more relieved when I told her that

I had met a wonderful girl and that I was going to join her law firm.

Uncle Don took the phone when I was done and gushed to Mom about how unbelievably astute I had been while in his employ and that the factory was now duly sold and no longer a worry to him.

I said goodbye to Uncle Don and drove back to my apartment.

Jennifer and I had arranged that she would stay over at my place each night beginning tonight while we looked for a suitable place to live in Alfred.

Today was the end of the line for my stint as a factory manager and part-time truck driver.

CHAPTER 29 (Finding a Home)

Jennifer arrived at five-thirty and we went to a restaurant to celebrate what was technically our first night of permanent cohabitation.

She was amazed when I disclosed the news that Uncle Don had given me a generous bonus.

We began discussing where we would like to live. Both of us preferred to reside right in Alfred in order to avoid commuting daily from any of the nearby towns or villages.

"It's possible that my landlord might be forced to evict me from my office," Jennifer mentioned.

"Why is that?"

"This Covid-19 pandemic has crushed his rental income. The retail store on the main floor failed to pay rent all spring and summer and promptly went out of business right after Labor Day. To make matters worse, the residential tenant on the third floor also stiffed Mr. Cranston on the rent for several months and flew the coop on the weekend. I've been the only tenant paying any rent and Mr. Cranston in going to be forced to sell the building."

The downtown area of Alfred was miniscule and consisted of one short block of very old commercial buildings on just one side of the main street. There were only about nine storefronts in those connected buildings and some of those businesses were vacant.

"Perhaps we could purchase the building and use it for both our office and residence," I commented.

"That's a possibility. As we've seen on the internet and driving around the village, there's virtually nothing for sale or rent right now. Alfred University students tend to snap up any available apartments."

"Have you ever seen the apartment on the third floor?"

"No."

"Does the building only consist of the single storefront, your office on the second storey and the apartment on the top floor?"

"That's right. It's not a very deep building and the apartment can only be accessed from the rear of the building."

"Your legal office would be a bit cramped if we both worked from there. There's barely enough room for you and your secretary."

"That's a good point. The retail area on the main floor seems to be quite a bit larger. We could move our office there and rent out my second floor office."

"Another option might be to turn your office into our living quarters and find another residential tenant for the top floor apartment."

"I like that idea. Tomorrow let's contact the owner and find out what price he's contemplating. If he's way out of line then we can strike that option off our list and look for alternatives."

On Wednesday morning we drove to Alfred since Jennifer had to work. She called her landlord, Gerald Cranston.

He was extremely interested in selling his building and we arranged to meet him at noon to inspect the storefront space and the third floor rear apartment.

Jennifer's secretary was not working today but Jennifer had no appointments scheduled so she put a sign on the door that she would return in an hour.

Mr. Cranston was an older gentleman in his seventies and he mentioned that he had owned the downtown building since 1982 when he had purchased it during a vicious economic recession when interest rates were sky high.

The rents he collected when the building was fully occupied ranged somewhat. Jennifer's office rent was $800 per month. The third floor apartment brought in $575 and the main floor retail space had been rented out at $1,200. Each of those rents included utilities because the various units were not separately metered.

The apartment was very basic and even smaller than Jennifer's office because the exterior stairway up to the apartment reduced the square footage of the third floor. It was a one-bedroom unit but each room was quite cramped.

The retail space was larger because it extended about twelve feet beyond the second and third storeys at the rear of the building.

Before we got around to dickering about price, we apprised Mr. Cranston of a few benefits from negotiating a quick sale to Jennifer and me.

For one thing, we could accommodate a very quick closing.

Also, we were willing to purchase the building even though it was vacant on the main and top floors.

Mr. Cranston admitted that he had encountered great difficulty in finding a reliable tenant for the apartment and seemed to get stuck with one deadbeat after another.

He also had poor luck with the storefront and had found that it generally took many months to find a new retail tenant whenever the unit became vacant. He added that the Covid-19 pandemic lockdowns likely meant that the storefront would remain vacant for a considerable time until the economy eventually got back to normal.

With those issues duly discussed, we began negotiating the sale price.

Cranston was no patsy and twice Jennifer and I declined his reduced offer, thanked him for his time and began to walk away.

Our tactic worked because his bottom line price dropped from $240,000 to $199,000 and finally to $169,900.

Jennifer and I went off by ourselves for a moment after Cranston made that last offer.

"The price now seems reasonable, Bobby. I think I can live with $169,900."

"It's a very old building and he's made it crystal clear that he's selling the place in an 'as is' condition. I noticed some water damage in the apartment and a flat roof often requires frequent resealing. I'd like to try for one more reduction."

We walked back to Mr. Cranston.

"The roof obviously leaks, sir. We've discussed your proposition and we've decided that we'd be willing to pay $165,000. The drop from your latest offer is solely because of the outlay we'd have to make immediately in order for the apartment to be habitable."

"I can't go that low. I'm sorry."

"We fully understand, Mr. Cranston. Again we thank you for taking the time to show us around the building. Jennifer and I will look at other properties in town or in nearby towns. We were both leery about taking on a century-old downtown structure."

Mr. Cranston thanked us for contacting him and we left the storefront and went up to Jennifer's office to determine how we could rearrange the set-up to accommodate me joining the firm.

Twenty minutes later Mr. Cranston appeared.

"I accept your offer of $165,000, kids. Even though I hate the price, everything else is perfect. I won't have to bust my rear end trying to find new tenants and I won't have the worry of unexpected repairs or vandalizing renters."

We prepared the purchase offer while Mr. Cranston called his own attorney. We set the closing date for December 10th.

Twenty minutes later we had signed the offer, written the deposit check to his lawyer in trust and then waited while Cranston attended at his own attorney's office a few blocks away.

Within another half hour,
Cranston had accepted the offer
and delivered back to us our
signed copies of the agreement.

One of the terms of the offer
was that we would take possession
of the third floor apartment
immediately which meant that while
Jennifer worked in her office for
the remainder of the week, I could
begin cleaning up the apartment
since the absconding tenant had
left the place in a bit of a mess.

I had no furniture at all but
Jennifer had her own belongings
stored in her parents' basement
and garage.

On Saturday we would rent a
small van and move Jennifer's
furniture into the third storey
apartment which would serve as our
temporary residence while we
completed a few renovations and
improvements to make the
storefront area suitable for our
legal office.

Until Saturday Jennifer and I
would sleep over at my Wellsville
apartment.

We ate a celebratory supper at a restaurant in Alfred and then dropped in to visit Jennifer's parents and give them our latest news.

CHAPTER 30 (Rosy Future)

The next ten days were frantic but quite wonderful.

While Jennifer ran her law office, I supervised renovations in the third floor apartment and in the storefront which would be our combined office.

By Friday the apartment sported a new paint job and new carpet which meant that on Saturday Jennifer and I moved in to freshly decorated temporary living quarters.

The storefront changes would be more extensive but Mr. Cranston gave us permission to commence the renovations immediately.

The purchase transaction closed as scheduled on Thursday, the 10th of December which meant that Jennifer and I were now the proud owners of an historic downtown Alfred building.

I made the required notifications in order to join

Jennifer's law firm but we decided that for the first couple of weeks I would assist the renovators rather than begin work as an attorney.

By Christmas the storefront had been transformed into a cheery law office and we made arrangements to move Jennifer's office furniture into the new location during the week after Christmas.

That move also went without a glitch.

We hired the same renovation outfit to transform the second floor office into an upscale residential unit.

Those improvements were expected to take about a month after which Jennifer and I would move in to a lovely apartment.

It would be incredibly handy managing a work commute of only fourteen steps from our apartment to our new law office.

Our plans also included getting married in a small civil ceremony in late February.

The New Year 2021 promised to be a magnificent year for the undercover trucker and the love of his life.

Life was definitely great.

THE END

ABOUT THE AUTHOR

Lance Majestik is the pen name of a retired Canadian lawyer who has written more than 100 novels, most of which have been published under his real name.

That mystery author decided to write a few shorter novels using the pen name Lance Majestik.

Please check out "Lance's" tiny portfolio of novels:

COLD CASE LAWYER

UNVACCINATED OLD LAWYER (Rebel Without a Jab)

OLD MIND, YOUNG BODY (Body Switch)

BETTER TIMES (A Comeback Story)

LOVE IN OLEAN (An American Romance)

UNDERCOVER TRUCKER (An American Mystery)

CRAZY OLD LAWYER (A Talking Skin Tag)

LOVE MOCKS A LIMP DICK (War of the Sexes)

P.S. To unlock the mystery, check out the Author Page on Amazon for Lance Majestik.

www.ingramcontent.com/pod-product-compliance
Lightning Source LLC
Chambersburg PA
CBHW060044150626
46556CB00018BA/2683